Hearts in Harmony

Dear ~~Mr. MacLean~~
I hope you enjoy reading this book
as much as I enjoyed writing it!
All the best,
Cassidy Lea

Cassidy Lea

ISBN 978-1-0980-1385-1 (paperback)
ISBN 978-1-0980-1386-8 (digital)

Christian Faith Publishing, Inc.
832 Park Avenue
Meadville, PA 16335
www.christianfaithpublishing.com

Printed in the United States of America

Acknowledgments

So many people played a part in making this book a reality, and I just want to take a moment to thank some of the people who made this all possible.

To Mom and Dad. Thank you for praying for me, encouraging me, and always being willing to listen to fragments of future stories. I love you both; thank you for showing me what God's love is like.

To my family, friends, and church family, thank you for believing in this crazy dream, for asking me about the book and encouraging me to keep working at it. Your love and support mean more than you know.

To the authors and proofreaders who gave me advice and helped me refine my ideas, thank you so much for sharing your expertise.

To my two favourite hockey players. Thanks for making the game special to me.

To the publishing specialists who have helped me along the way, thank you for your patience in walking me through this process.

And finally, all praise be to God, who brings all that He starts into completion.

Chapter One

Fingering the cross that hung on a chain around her neck, Harmony Clark sat in the backseat of a cab, marveling at the extravagant homes that dotted the landscape as the cab rolled up the tree-lined drive. Harmony's jaw dropped as the cab driver turned into a long driveway that revealed a stunning mansion against a picturesque backdrop of large evergreen trees and the distant snow-capped Rocky Mountains.

There had to be some mistake, some dreadful, laughingly ridiculous mistake. After spending years working as a missionary in Indonesia, Harmony had returned to Canada, the country of her birth, in order to help a struggling family. This could *not* be where Kyle Taylor, her soon-to-be boss, and his family lived. She had flown over ten thousand kilometres to come back to Canada and driven an hour outside of her hometown of Calgary all to help a family in *need*. She was obviously in the wrong place.

"Are you sure this is the right address?" Harmony asked the cab driver, feeling like Alice must have felt when she landed in Wonderland. This was not what she pictured when she thought of a family in need—not even close.

"Yes, Ma'am, this is the place," the cab driver affirmed, letting out a low whistle. "Pretty fancy set-up they got here."

You're telling me, Harmony thought to herself, craning her neck to see around the enormous mansion. To the back of the lot, she could just make out a small bungalow that was simple but in good condition.

That must be where Kyle and his family live, she thought with a sigh of relief. Kyle and his wife probably worked long hours in that big house, so they needed her to take care of their daughter while they were busy in the mansion. Harmony struggled to remember the information her mother had given her about Kyle Taylor's family. Marjorie Taylor, Kyle's mother, had been Harmony's mother's roommate in university, and Marjorie had definitely not mentioned any mansions.

Harmony thanked and paid the cab driver then slowly approached the ridiculously large home, trailing her suitcase—her only suitcase—behind her and wondering what type of person needed a house that size. Glancing to her right, Harmony saw a burly middle-aged man with greying temples, who looked as if he could use a few hours more shut-eye, mowing the lawn. Well, at least Kyle Taylor was a hands-on kind of guy. Harmony squinted in the sun, trying to see him better.

Surely, that man couldn't be Marjorie's son. Harmony knew that Marjorie was the same age as her mother, and this man looked to be the same age or older!

Harmony frowned. Then again, stress and hard work had a way of aging a person. That theory wasn't very convincing, but she left her bag on the driveway and approached the man rather warily before he noticed her and stopped the lawn mower. Harmony extended her hand and introduced herself, giving the man a sunny smile.

"Hello, my name is Harmony Clark. You must be… Mr. Taylor?"

The man smiled and shook her hand. "It's nice to meet you, Miss Clark, but I'm not Kyle Taylor." Harmony was not entirely surprised but hurried to cover up her embarrassment.

"Oh, I'm so sorry, I just assumed…"

The man laughed and shook his head. "It's all right, I just work here," the man smiled. "My name is Abraham Wright. I'm the maintenance man." He pointed to the bungalow that she had seen when the taxi had driven up. "My wife and I live right in that house over there."

There goes that theory.

Abraham paused for a minute, studying her. "So, I guess you've never seen a picture of Kyle Taylor, huh?"

Harmony narrowed her eyes at him, thoroughly confused. "Marjorie didn't send me any pictures…"

Abraham stifled a chuckle. "Well, all right then, why don't you just come inside?"

Abraham grabbed Harmony's bag and led her around the side of the mansion to the kitchen mudroom entrance. A short salt-and-pepper-haired lady greeted them once inside. She was wearing a pristine white apron that didn't show evidence of any cooking; however, the aromas in the room completely contradicted the spotlessness of the kitchen. Harmony almost felt self-conscious standing before a woman who was just as dignified as the queen of England. Abraham placed a kiss on the woman's cheek before gesturing towards Harmony.

"This is Harmony Clark. Harmony, this is my wife Clarissa. You will find she reigns over this kitchen with an iron spatula," Abraham said with a cheeky grin. Clarissa smiled and shook Harmony's hand.

"Ah yes, it's a pleasure to meet you, dear. Now you," Clarissa said, turning to Abraham, planting her hands on her slender hips, and staring him down, "why on earth did you bring her through the kitchen entrance?"

"What do you mean? I always come in the kitchen entrance."

Clarissa rolled her eyes. "Men," she said playfully, shaking her head and mumbling something about not bringing guests through the kitchen entrance before she turned back to Harmony. "Why don't I show you to Mr. Taylor's office?"

Harmony followed Clarissa into an enormous, elegant foyer with a spiraling staircase that made her gasp. If this was only the foyer, what did the rest of the house look like? And what kind of person was Kyle Taylor if he could afford a house like this, along with a maintenance man and a housekeeper? And why would his daughter need a nanny to top it all off?

"This place is huge," Harmony gasped. "How do you keep up with it all?"

Clarissa shrugged. "Oh, I have a girl come in twice a week to help me with all the cleaning and such."

"Oh," Harmony nodded, trying to wrap her brain around the fact that Kyle Taylor had hired help who hired help. *Oh boy.* Harmony had never felt more ill at ease. She had spent most of her life living in one of the poorest communities in Indonesia. She could handle poverty, but this? This was excessive. *Lord, I don't know what on earth You're doing here, but please help me to trust that You've got a reason for calling me here.*

Harmony was led through the foyer into the hall where Clarissa knocked lightly on a huge mahogany door and opened it to reveal a large office with a small sitting area, an ornate desk, and four floor-to-ceiling bookcases complete with a ladder that could be pulled across so that one could reach the top shelves.

The thing that caught Harmony's eye, however, was the man sitting at the desk. He had dark brown wavy hair, chocolate brown eyes, and a well-built frame. He was no doubt very tall, well over six feet. At nearly five-nine, Harmony was tall for a woman, but she could still imagine only coming up to about his chin. Drop-dead gorgeous just didn't do him justice.

The thought caught Harmony so off guard that she cringed, waves of guilt threatening to drown her. How *dare* she think that way about her new boss—her married boss nonetheless. *Okay, okay,* she lectured herself. *You need to stop. So, he's good looking. Just keep in mind he's your new boss. And he's married.* She took a deep breath, battling a sudden feeling of sadness. *Besides, you're still in love with Roger.* Squaring her shoulders, she walked purposefully towards the man sitting at the desk.

Chapter Two

"Kyle, this is Harmony Clark to see you," Clarissa introduced them.

Kyle was concentrating on some paperwork when he became aware of the beautiful blond woman with gorgeous Caribbean blue eyes standing in front of him with an outstretched hand. He was not quite sure what to think. She was young-looking, probably a couple years younger than himself. She was tall but curvy, and she was wearing a simple outfit of jeans, a white blouse, and a blue cardigan. She had a more genuine, wholesome look to her than that of most women that he seemed to run into lately, even with the dark circles of fatigue framing her eyes. He glanced at Clarissa's retreating figure, wondering why everyone else seemed to know something that he didn't. Why did things like this always happen to him?

"I'm Harmony Clark. Nice to meet you, Mr. Taylor."

Kyle shook her hand, still trying to figure out what she was doing here. "Um, yes, can I help you?"

Harmony looked at him blankly, brushing a lock of hair behind her ear. "I'm the new nanny."

"What?" Kyle sputtered. "Who hired you?"

Harmony bit her lip and fumbled with the simple gold cross that hung across her neck. "Your mother, Marjorie Taylor. You didn't know?"

Kyle groaned. He should have known that his mother would be at the bottom of this. He sighed, vaguely remembering his mother mentioning that she'd hired a woman who—how did she put it?— "would be a perfect addition to our family."

"Oh, that Harmony Clark. I, ah, wasn't expecting you so soon." He motioned Harmony towards a chair.

Harmony sat down in one of the chairs in front of his desk. "I'm sorry if I mixed up the dates. I was sure that Marjorie said to come today."

Kyle sighed again and mumbled, "No, this won't work."

Harmony didn't appear to have heard him as she asked him a question. "Your mother hired me, but we didn't discuss the details such as salary or time off, although she did say that I'd be provided with living arrangements. Oh, and I look forward to meeting your wife."

Kyle's hand stilled as he went to run it through his hair. He looked at her sharply.

"My wife? What are you talking about?"

"Um, I, uh," Harmony's hand flew back to the cross at her neck, "your daughter's mother?"

"Oh," Kyle narrowed his eyes, giving the woman across from him a hard stare. "Her mother's not in the picture," he stated while red flags were going off in his mind at the woman's question. Because of his hockey career, privacy was not a thing that he could count on, and in the three years since his daughter Ellie had been born, he had been subject to both censure and hero worship because of his status as a single dad. He found it hard to believe that this Harmony woman didn't already know that about him.

He had to give her credit though; the innocent act was convincing, but he'd dealt with enough women who were only interested in his career as a National Hockey League player to be fooled by another pretty face. Even if that wasn't the case, she was definitely trouble with a capital T, and judging by the cute way she bit her lip when she was worried matched with her breathtaking blue eyes, she would prove to be only one thing: a distraction. And a distraction was not what Kyle needed right now.

"Should we discuss salary and time off?" Harmony asked, clearly embarrassed by the carelessness, albeit accidental, of her earlier question.

Though Kyle didn't believe the sincerity of this woman, when he looked into her clear blue eyes, he was struck by the sadness that lurked in their depths. And that got to him.

He sighed and picked up his cheque book, reaching for a pen. He knew how this thing worked, but he was surprised at the realization that he'd wanted her to be different.

"How much do you want?" Kyle asked her.

Harmony looked startled. "You mean salary-wise?"

Kyle suppressed the urge to roll his eyes. *Way to play it innocently.* "Come on, don't play that card with me. Do you really want to be a nanny for the next thirteen years or so?"

Harmony looked especially confused, and her fingers ran over the necklace for the umpteenth time. "Well, I don't know if I can commit to thirteen years, but for the foreseeable future, yes. Isn't that why I'm here?" she asked.

Kyle clenched his jaw, wishing that for once he could trust a woman to be honest with him. "Do you know who I am?"

She smiled at him warily. "Kyle Taylor?" she asked with lifted brows.

"What do I do for a living?"

"Ah, you haven't told me yet."

He leaned forward in his chair wondering where in the world this woman came from. Granted he'd only just been traded to Calgary from Ottawa during the off season, but still, most people would at least know a famous hockey player if they saw one, especially in Canada.

"I play hockey," Kyle stated, hoping to ring some bells.

"And?" she questioned.

"What do you mean *and*?"

Harmony tilted her head to one side, giving him a questioning look. "Well, what do you do for a living?"

Did she really just ask him that? Okay, she had to be an alien. Anyone from practically anywhere would know that people played hockey for a living, and no woman in her right mind—no matter how manipulative—would ever *pretend* she didn't know that one could play hockey for a living.

"Where did you say you were from?" Kyle just had to ask.

"I was born in Calgary, but my parents are missionaries in Indonesia so I mostly grew up there. Actually, my plane just landed this morning."

Kyle nodded in understanding. *Well, that explains a lot.*

"Are we going to discuss my salary now?" Harmony asked patiently.

"Oh yeah, right." *Get back on track, Taylor,* Kyle silently directed himself. He supposed that since she apparently wasn't going to leave, he might as well give her the ground rules.

"You will be living here in the house because Ellie will need you for most of every day. You will stay out of my stuff—that means my room, my office, my mail, etcetera. As to your salary"—Kyle quickly scribbled out a number on a piece of paper and slid it across the desk towards her. He couldn't help but hope that she would be aghast at the amount and demand more. He, of course, would not be offering anything extra, so it would end with her leaving in a huff and him back to trying to find a *suitable* nanny. He eyed her from across the desk. Emphasis on suitable.

Harmony looked like her eyes were about to pop out of her head and she gawked up at him. "You want to pay me *that* much?"

Great, wrong reaction.

"I couldn't possibly accept such a high salary."

Okay, so this plan might work after all. "I think it's a reasonable wage, but if you won't accept it, I guess I'll have to let you go," Kyle stared at her with a challenge in his eyes. Maybe, just maybe, she would fall into the trap. He needed someone less...well, less like the woman in front of him. Kyle watched as she considered—one hand holding the paper with her salary, the other holding the cross at her neck. *Missionary's kid huh,* Kyle thought, cocking his head to one side. *Interesting.*

"Well, you know, it all really depends on whether or not you can work with my daughter," Kyle smirked, and at that moment, his mother and daughter walked into the office along with the family ferret, Mookie. Kyle sat back in his chair. Here was the ultimate test, whether or not his daughter liked this woman and if Harmony could handle having a ferret in the house.

His daughter Elora, commonly known as Ellie, half-hid behind his mother's legs. She peeked out from behind Marjorie and glanced at him quickly before gazing at the pretty stranger.

"Ellie, this is my new friend Miss Harmony," his mother introduced them. "Harmony, this is my amazingly wonderful granddaughter that I told you about, Ellie." Harmony smiled and waved at the little girl, and Ellie looked up questioningly at her grandmother.

"Go on," Marjorie encouraged. "Say hello."

Ellie took a tentative step out from behind Marjorie, and Harmony slid off the chair to kneel down in front of her.

"Hi, Ellie, I'm Harmony."

Ellie was holding Mookie in her arms—close to her chest—when she walked over to Harmony and thrust the ferret towards her.

Kyle nearly fell off his chair. Ellie never went anywhere near strangers. Why, she was barely comfortable with family. Even more surprising was that Harmony took Mookie from her and held him close.

"What is this little fella's name?" Harmony gazed with interest at his daughter, cradling an animal Kyle could only consider a glorified rat. At least she seemed to take a genuine interest in Ellie.

"Mookie," his daughter replied, "I named him mysewf." Ellie hesitated a moment before tentatively grabbing Harmony's arm and gently pulling her to her feet. "My name is actually Ewora, but evewybody calls me Elwie," she dragged Harmony towards the door. "Come and I will show you mine and Mookie's woom."

Kyle stared absolutely speechless as he watched them leave the room. He could barely maintain a five-minute conversation with his daughter then some nanny shows up and Ellie suddenly talks a mile per minute? Was it a miracle, or was Kyle setting himself up for another disappointment?

Marjorie turned towards him. "So…are you going to thank me?"

Finally, Kyle found his voice, making a concentrated effort to keep his jaw from going slack. "Thank you? Thank you that you hired a woman who will be taking care of *my* daughter without *my* permission? Thank you that you hired a nanny who will most likely not last a year? I mean look at her: She's young and beautiful. Do you really think she'll want to be tied down as a nanny to a little girl for the next several years? Don't you think she will want to, I don't know, get married? Have a life?"

Kyle clenched his jaw, trying to keep the bitterness out of his voice. He couldn't help being cynical. He was used to people trying to get close to him for money or fame, but if anyone thought they could use Ellie to get to him, they were sorely mistaken. He wouldn't let anyone hurt Ellie.

What really had him worried was the fact that he had known Harmony for all of fifteen minutes and he had already fallen under her spell. Not only because of her looks—though he could not deny that she was a very beautiful woman—but the way she tipped her head slightly when she smiled, the way she spoke to his daughter, the fact that she didn't scream and stand on the chair the moment she saw Mookie. And the sadness that hid behind her sunny smile. Kyle glanced down at his watch. Had it really only been fifteen minutes?

Before he started off again, his mother silenced him with raised eyebrows. His mother had always been blunt, but since having cancer, she never minced words or beat around the bush. "I think," she said in a huff, "that you're just mad because I did such a good job finding you a nanny. She has all the qualities you asked for."

"Yeah, except the 'old and homely' part," Kyle grumbled, only half under his breath.

"Oh, grow up and get your hormones under control," Marjorie snapped. "You are a twenty-nine-year-old man, not some testoster-one-crazed teenager. You should be able to have a beautiful woman around and control yourself."

Boy, did he hate it when she did that to him. Only his mother possessed the power to make him feel like some naughty five-year-old caught with his hand in the cookie jar. Kyle rolled his eyes. "Mom, of course I can control myself. After all, who said anything about her being beautiful?"

Marjorie looked at him pointedly. "You did."

"Did not."

"Whatever. But she is gorgeous, isn't she? And Ellie loves her already. Plus, I have a feeling this will work out wonderfully"—she paused, looking at him archly—"if you cooperate." After a moment of silence, she asked with a sly grin in his direction, "So do you want me to give her the grand tour?"

Kyle sighed and pinched the bridge of his nose. He could tell by his mother's tone of voice that she meant business. He backed down. "Fine, show her around. Whatever, I don't care. You'll be mostly responsible for supervising her anyway," he turned back to his work as his mother exited his office.

Chapter Three

Harmony's mind was a whirl as she only half-listened to Ellie's cheerful babbling. *What had happened with Ellie's mother?* She didn't think the woman had passed away, but she wondered what could have happened to have driven a woman to leave her daughter or a man to keep a mother away from her daughter. Harmony smiled at the back of Ellie's head. *And such a lovely daughter at that.*

And what did Kyle mean by "I play hockey"? Here she was thinking she would be lending a hand to some overworked, financially tight family that needed some able-bodied person to care for their child. Boy, was she mistaken.

Ellie led the way through a hallway, up a flight of stairs, through another hallway, and finally into a pretty pink bedroom that had to be hers. It had white wood furniture, and the bed was inset into the wall with bookcases around it and pink sheer curtains that could be opened or closed around the head of the bed. There was a pink window seat and a fuzzy pink carpet on the floor. Her dresser had a mirror attached to it that was decorated with pink butterfly stickers and a fluffy pink scarf glued around the outside.

It was just a hunch, but Harmony was certain that Ellie's favourite colour was pink. Ellie made her way towards a little pink castle and gently pushed Mookie into the window of the tallest tower. Then she turned to Harmony and motioned towards her room.

"Do you wike it?"

Harmony smiled, noticing that Ellie had a cute little lisp when pronouncing words with *l* and *r*. Harmony nodded. "I love it."

Just at that moment, the door opened and Marjorie came in smiling. "Ellie, honey, Clarissa has a snack for you in the kitchen and I have to show Miss Harmony around, okay?"

Ellie's face fell a little bit. "Does she have to weave?" she asked, stepping closer to Harmony and gazing up at her, her golden curls framing her cherub-like face.

"Actually," Marjorie explained, leading the way out the door, "Miss Harmony's going to be your new nanny."

"Yay!"

With her curls bouncing, Ellie gave Harmony a quick hug around the knees before running off to the kitchen.

Marjorie motioned to Harmony. "Come with me and I'll show you around. I've already had Abraham take your bags to your room so I'll give you the grand tour."

Harmony smiled, pushing a lock of hair behind her ear. "I'm glad you came. I don't think I would have been able to find my way back downstairs if you hadn't."

Marjorie just laughed.

"Grand tour" was a total understatement. Marjorie showed her the theater room, the games room, the family room, the dining room, the guest rooms, the exercise room, the sauna, and the indoor pool, then led her to the giant patio and outdoor skating rink located behind the house.

Harmony's heart had stalled when they'd passed the indoor pool. There were no locks on the doors and she had a sinking feeling that Ellie didn't know how to swim. It would be far too easy for the young girl to slip into the room unsupervised. Harmony filed the information in the back of her mind, determined to talk to Kyle about it when she had the chance and try to forget the reason why it bothered her so much.

"How do you keep the skating rink, well, icy when we're barely at the end of August?" Harmony asked Marjorie curiously as they passed the rink.

"Oh, we use synthetic ice," Marjorie stated casually.

"Oh, right."

Well, that was clear as mud. Although Harmony supposed that might be a given to anyone who knew anything about outdoor skating rinks, whatever Kyle meant by "I play hockey," he was obviously pretty serious about it, having his own personal skating rink.

Next, Marjorie showed her a complete playground set for Ellie. The playground had pink swings, pink monkey bars, and a pink slide. Harmony couldn't help but wonder how they managed that. They reentered the house, and Marjorie led her up the stairs and back in the direction of Ellie's room.

"Here is your room."

Harmony's eyes widened at the opulent-looking room with a blue bed set and white curtains. A television, dresser, and bedside table along with a cozy window seat with lush pillows, perfect for curling up with a good book, made up the rest of the room. "You'll be sharing the jack-and-jill bathroom with Ellie since her room is just beside yours."

Harmony stood in a daze, trying to keep her jaw from dropping to the floor. "This is perfect, Thank you. This is more than I could ever dream of."

Her room on the mission field had consisted of a small cot, a few shelves, and hooks for her things. Harmony shook her head in disbelief. *For good or for bad, you've come a long way, baby.*

Marjorie beamed. "Oh, it's nothing. I've been praying about this for a long time, and I think you will be exactly what this place needs." With that, Marjorie left the room.

*****

Harmony could not have been happier in a job than she was now, and she praised God that things were working out so well. She had been working at the Taylor House—more like Mansion—for nearly three weeks. She attended church with Marjorie and Ellie, and it had not taken much time at all for her to decide that Ellie was the sweetest little girl she'd ever met. Like all children, she definitely had her moments, but Harmony had discovered that she was a caring, bubbly, and sensitive three-year-old and Harmony loved taking care of her. They were having a lot of fun together and Harmony was beginning to think that her father had been right when he had counseled her to take this job.

Harmony also discovered that Kyle was a "professional" hockey player, and therefore, it was a career. The only concern she had was that Kyle didn't seem to be too involved with Ellie. He left all her care to either Harmony or his mother. He was always busy practising and doing whatever else professional hockey players do, and it was only late August. By the time the hockey season rolled around, Harmony doubted she'd see him at all.

It wasn't as if she really minded; in reality, it made Harmony's job much easier. She'd like to deny the fact that every time she saw him, a million butterflies took flight in her stomach, but nothing could be further from the truth. It was probably because he was her boss, and in direct supervision of how she worked whenever he was home. Harmony scoffed. Even she didn't believe that. More than likely, she was still adjusting to sharing a house with a man her age, since she had no brothers. Anyway, just because Kyle made her uncomfortable didn't mean that Ellie shouldn't get to see her dad.

Harmony sighed, feeling a twinge of guilt. It wasn't like her to be so uncharitable. She hadn't been able to stop thinking about Ellie's mother. Kyle had been so vague and Marjorie was extremely tight-lipped about the whole thing. All Harmony knew was that the woman apparently didn't want to be a part of Ellie's life. Or Kyle's. That would be hard on anyone. Armed with the determination to be easier on Kyle, Harmony gave herself one last look in the mirror, smoothed on a little lip balm, and headed to the kitchen.

Harmony had never really believed that the kitchen was, in fact, the heart of the home, but considering how much time they all spent there, she'd been proved wrong. Ellie was already seated, eating her breakfast along with someone Harmony had never seen before. She gave the young man a once-over. He looked to be about Kyle's age, a bit shorter than him, with shaggy sandy-brown hair and moss-green eyes. He was very handsome and radiated boyish charm.

When he glanced up, Harmony held out her hand. "Hi there. My name is Harmony Clark. I'm Ellie's new nanny." She smiled as he gave her a lopsided grin, shaking her hand.

"It's a pleasure to meet you. I'm Lucas Nelson," he introduced himself, his green eyes sparkling. "I play hockey with Kyle."

Within minutes, they were chatting away like old friends. Lucas asked her numerous questions about her family, and she quickly discovered that he had a great sense of humour. When she mentioned that she had been a missionary, he revealed that he had been raised in church and missed it but could not seem to find the time lately. They talked easily, and Harmony laughed till her sides hurt.

What surprised her most was that she kept looking at the doorway, wondering where Kyle was. She couldn't figure out why it would matter so much to her; he only ever made her uncomfortable anyway. Glancing at the little girl quietly eating breakfast next to her, Harmony realized that it was important to her because it was something that affected little Ellie. And anything that mattered to Ellie mattered to Harmony.

Kyle came into the kitchen only to see Lucas and Harmony having a cozy little confab while his daughter ate her breakfast. *Great.* Kyle clenched his jaw, momentarily taken aback by the irrational surge of jealousy that ran through him. What did it matter to him who Harmony chose to shower undue affection upon? He winced at the bitterness of the thought. *Back off, Taylor.* Nope, it didn't matter to him one bit, not one bit. It didn't bother him at all that neither of them so much as looked up when he came in. It didn't even bother him when neither acknowledged his presence when he grabbed a protein shake from the fridge and leaned back against the counter.

"Ahem," Kyle cleared his throat. Still no reaction. Nothing. Kyle clenched and unclenched his jaw. Okay, so he'd be a bit more direct this time. *Even though it doesn't bother me at all,* Kyle thought when he looked back at Lucas and Harmony sitting there, making googly eyes at each other. *Okay, so maybe it does bother me.* "So, Lucas," Kyle began, "what exactly are you doing here?"

"Is that any way to greet your friend after he's been away for three weeks?" Lucas might have been answering Kyle, but his smile and his gaze were directed at Harmony. "Besides, it's Thursday. We always go for a run on Thursday mornings."

Kyle nodded. "Okay," he said, "and this requires you to chat up my employee. Why?"

Lucas's head snapped up at his words. "Excuse me?"

At the same time, Harmony choked and sputtered on her coffee. Now he had their attention. "And you," Kyle said, turning his attention to Harmony, who was still smothering her coughs, "little miss sweetness and light, what are you thinking, flirting with my friend in front of my daughter."

Harmony flushed bright scarlet and hastily got up from her seat. "I... I wasn't flirting," she said in a tight, strained voice. She turned to Lucas, "Or at least I didn't mean to be. I would never want you to get the wrong idea. I...I'm sorry."

Lucas shook his head, shooting a glare in Kyle's direction. "You have nothing to apologize for. Don't worry about it."

Harmony smiled her thanks. She turned to Kyle, not quite meeting his gaze. "I'll just take Ellie to play now, if that's all right with you," she asked quietly. After his curt nod, they slipped from the room.

Kyle couldn't understand the woman. She was so nice she made him feel bad. And how was any of this his fault? He wasn't the one flirting in front of a three-year-old.

Kyle downed his protein drink in only a few gulps, not at all liking the cold glare he was receiving from Lucas.

Once Lucas was sure that Harmony and Ellie were out of earshot, he turned to Kyle and looked as if he was ready to punch Kyle's head into the wall. "What was that about? Why did you have to be so rude to her? I mean, seriously, you were a total jerk."

"Listen, she's *my* employee, so really, it's none of your business how I treat my staff," Kyle shot back defensively, already feeling like the scum of the earth for the way he'd spoken to Harmony.

"Well, it's *my* business, Kyle Anthony Taylor!" Marjorie said, bursting into the room. "What was the meaning of that?"

Kyle folded his arms across his chest. He'd felt bad enough when Harmony just apologized and left the room. She didn't get angry. She didn't come up with some smarty comeback or rude comment. At least if she'd done that, he'd feel like less of a jerk. Being harangued by his mother certainly wasn't going to help.

21

"Didn't I raise you better than that? Not only were you rude to your best friend, you accused Harmony—who is probably the sweetest woman alive—of flirting, as if that was some unpardonable sin!"

With her voice rising with every syllable, Marjorie continued, "Need I remind you that simply speaking to the opposite gender does not equate to flirting?" Wagging her finger in Kyle's face, she went on. "And even if she was flirting, as you so delicately put it, in front of a three-year-old, I doubt that would be the thing that would warp your daughter! As if you have never flirted with a woman in front of her before! You do understand that Harmony has committed to spending almost all her time with Ellie, so we have to let her make friends and get comfortable here, and even flirt if the mood strikes, and since you are not her father, you cannot forbid her from dating!"

Out of the corner of his eye, Kyle could see Lucas grinning like a cat that ate the canary. "Mom, you weren't even in the room. You didn't see them making 'googly eyes' at each other," Kyle said, casting a glare at Lucas.

Marjorie placed her hands on her slim hips. "I was just in the laundry room and I can hear perfectly well from down there, even if you do think I'm a doddering old woman."

Kyle snapped his mouth shut. Great. Now she was twisting his words too.

"Now you two are going on that run, and you, mister," she said, pointing at Kyle, "are going to make things right with Lucas and apologize to poor Harmony. Now go on, both of you."

Kyle turned to Lucas as they left the house, swallowing his pride or at least trying to. "I, uh, I'm sorry for freaking out at you in there," Kyle mumbled. Saying he was sorry didn't always come naturally for him. No, scratch that. It never did.

"It's all right, man," Lucas replied. After a brief pause, he continued, "But you've got to admit she is pretty cute."

Kyle grimaced. "Don't even go there. She looks after my kid."

Lucas shrugged, grinning.

"So, we're good?"

"Yeah, we're good. Let's just get going and forget about the whole thing," Lucas started jogging, a sly grin spreading across his face. "But would it be okay for me to ask her out?"

Kyle gave him a shove and rolled his eyes. "Don't even start with me."

Chapter Four

Harmony was distracted for the rest of the morning. How *could* Kyle have been so cruel? Little miss sweetness and light. He said it like it was a bad thing. And why did he get so freaked out over her talking to one of his hockey friends? And how could he accuse her of flirting?

She wasn't a flirt, and even if she *had* been flirting, was it any of his business? The more she thought about it, the angrier she became. Who did that man think he was, anyway? What made him think he deserved an opinion on her social life? Of all the rude, selfish, controlling…

Taking a moment to breathe, Harmony was reminded of a verse in Ephesians: "Be angry, yet do not sin." Because sin and anger often went hand in hand, Harmony mainly tried not to get angry.

Putting aside her hurt feelings, Harmony tried to think objectively. Had she been flirting? No, she wasn't a flirt. Was she? Harmony thought over her conversation with Lucas. She was sure that she was simply being friendly. Lucas didn't seem to think that she'd been flirting. Then what had given Kyle the idea that she had been? And why should his opinion matter to her anyway? Especially when he made such a fuss over her talking to one of his friends. Glancing at Ellie, Harmony's cheeks heated. She couldn't believe that the whole fiasco had taken place with Ellie in the room. Ugh, what a great nanny she was turning out to be.

Ellie's voice pulled her from her thoughts.

"Can we pwease watch a movie now?"

Harmony smiled. "Anything for you, princess."

She reached forward and tickled Ellie's ear. The little girl giggled and scooted away while Harmony put in her newest Christian DVD. When the movie ended, Harmony took Ellie to play. After helping the little girl tie her shoes, she hustled Ellie outside and onto the play set. Harmony pushed Ellie on the swing for a while then they had races from the ground to the top of Ellie's "tower," as she called it.

"Miss Hawmony?" Ellie had climbed to the top of her tower and was looking down at her, her golden curls flying out haphazardly from her face.

"Yes, Ellie?"

"Can we go to da water park?"

Harmony paused, considering. She hadn't taken Ellie off the grounds before, and she wasn't sure if she had to ask permission or not.

"Well, we'd have to ask your daddy. Why don't we do that right now?" Harmony really wasn't looking forward to asking Kyle for any favours after what had happened that morning, but hey, it was for Ellie. Besides, he wouldn't bring it up again in front of Ellie, would he? She looked up to find Ellie staring at her, her arms crossed in front of her chest and her lower lip sticking out.

"What's wrong, sweetie?"

Ellie shook her head, tears welling in her eyes. "I don't wanna ask Daddy."

"Why not? Honey, what's wrong?" Harmony grabbed Ellie from her playset, holding her close.

"I don't know what to say!" Ellie wailed, bursting into tears.

Harmony was completely taken aback. Did Kyle not even have time to speak to his daughter? Harmony thought of her own childhood. Aside from her twin sister, her parents had always been her best friends. Her heart ached for the poor little girl who barely knew her father.

"Shhh, it's okay, honey. You're fine," Harmony cooed softly to her. "You're going to be just fine."

She gently rocked Ellie back and forth, rubbing her back all the while. Once Ellie had calmed down, Harmony took her inside to ask Marjorie to go to the water park instead. Harmony sighed as she watched Ellie run to Marjorie and eagerly explain what she wanted. Much as she didn't want to, Harmony needed to talk to Kyle.

*****

After Harmony had made sure that Ellie was all right and eating lunch with her grandma, she made her way down the hall to Kyle's office. She knocked on the door and entered when she heard a "come in" from the other side. She closed the door behind her and walked towards the desk. Kyle was sitting there, looking mildly surprised to see her, his brown hair tousled and damp from a recent shower. Not that she was paying that much attention.

"I would like to talk to you about something. Actually, about a few things." Harmony tried her best not to think about how good looking Kyle was, mentally listing off all the reasons why he wasn't right for her. Aside from that, she had no right to think of him as anything other than her boss, and she would do well to remember that.

Kyle sat back in his chair, his brown eyes intense and his arms crossed over his chest. Oh yes, this was bound to go splendidly.

"Okay," he said slowly as he waited for her to continue.

"I was, uh, wondering if I could talk to you about a few things that have sort of been bothering me." Harmony braved a brief glance up and immediately regretted it. Well, he certainly wasn't making this any easier for her. At least his piercing gaze distracted her from the flecks of gold in his chocolate-brown eyes. She cringed a little at the irony of that thought, focusing instead on the intricate detailing on the front of his desk.

Frankly, she didn't want to have to talk to him at all; being around him set her on edge. Her stomach was aflutter with a million butterflies, her hands were clammy, and she had a nearly irresistible urge to smooth back her hair, which was absolutely ridiculous, considering the way he had acted that morning.

"Harmony." Kyle's voice was surprisingly gentle. Harmony looked up only to find him gazing at her with compassion, remorse, and…something else. Admiration, maybe? But why?

"If this is about this morning," Kyle trailed off, running his fingers through his hair. "I... I'm sorry. I shouldn't have reacted that way and accused you of..." He trailed off again and avoided her gaze. Was he blushing? "Well, I'm sorry. Is there anything else you wanted to talk to me about?"

"Actually, there was." Harmony regarded Kyle in a new light. There was definitely more to him than met the eye. "I was wondering if Ellie knew how to swim."

Kyle gave her a look. "She's three. Of course she doesn't know how to swim."

"Well, that's not actually that young to start learning to swim. I mean, the pool is just downstairs, no locks on the doors." Harmony shook her head. "I thought that maybe I could teach her," she began, then corrected herself, formulating an idea in her head. "Actually, I was wondering if you would like to help me teach her."

Kyle shook his head. "I have no time. Hockey season is starting up soon. I have my assets to take care of, my investments, the list goes on. I don't have time to teach her to swim."

Harmony immediately bristled at the callous way he spoke about spending time with his daughter. "Maybe you should make time," she snapped. Harmony bit her tongue and took a deep breath. Talking back to her boss was a no-no. She tried again, making a point to be as calm and as reasonable as possible. "I just think that she would really benefit from any extra time you can spend with her. Besides," Harmony said softly, "she only gets to be young once so..." Harmony sighed. "Don't cheat her out of the moments that she could be spending with her dad."

Kyle glared at her from behind his desk, his jaw clenched and his voice cold. "You can go now."

Harmony gritted her teeth. She'd crossed the line. She just hoped it wasn't Ellie who suffered for it.

Kyle stayed in his office the remainder of the afternoon and evening. He couldn't get any more work done after Harmony's visit. He could barely get to sleep that night. He figured she was right about the swimming lessons, but that wasn't what had been keeping him awake tonight.

What did Harmony mean when she said, "Don't cheat her out of the moments that she could be spending with her dad?" Why did it matter anyway? Ellie was only three, she probably wouldn't remember most of her early years anyway. He grunted and rolled over in bed. And yet he knew that it did matter. Of course, it mattered. Ellie mattered. He just…he just wasn't such great dad material. And how was he supposed to know what it takes to be a good father? It wasn't like he'd had such a great example.

Kyle sighed again. He loved Ellie, but that didn't mean he knew what to do with her. He'd been thrown into fatherhood with no time to prepare, and even three years later, it seemed as though he had yet to get a grip on everything. He sat up and punched his pillow a few times before lying back down. Should he take Harmony's advice and help teach Ellie to swim?

Ever since Ellie had been born she'd had a nanny, and now, suddenly, the new one seemed to think that *he* should be the one spending time with her. None of the others had ever said something like that to him. Besides, he was the one signing their cheques. Maybe the others just hadn't cared that much. He got up, frustrated, and threw his pillow across the room. He groaned and ran his fingers through his hair. He was never going to get to sleep like this. He needed to calm down and clear his head.

Kyle slipped a sweater over his T-shirt and put on a pair of jeans. He left his room and made his way downstairs, grabbing his skates, hockey stick, and a bag of hockey pucks that he'd left near the back-door. He exited the house and sat on a bench by the skating rink to put on his skates.

Flipping on the floodlights surrounding the ice, he set up the hockey pucks parallel to one of the nets. Skating on synthetic ice was different from skating on real ice, but being able to skate in the convenience of his own home made it an acceptable substitute. He shot one puck after the other, skated around the rink, deked to the left, shot, and scored! While skating always cleared his head, it didn't seem to be working so well now. He skated around the rink, forwards, backwards, took a couple shots. Nothing was helping. Growing more and more agitated, he threw down his hockey stick, breathing heavily.

What was wrong with him? He wasn't doing anything wrong! Ellie was having all her needs met. She lived in a big house and had all the toys a kid could dream of, even her own playground in the backyard, for goodness' sake. Why was it such a big deal that he wasn't around a lot, or that even when he was, he wasn't spending the time with her, or the rest of his family for that matter?

Kyle was so worked up that he tripped over his own feet and landed hard on his side on the ice. It took him a couple of minutes to catch his breath. He moaned and turned onto his back, looking up at the barely visible stars from under the floodlights. If only he still believed everything he'd learned about God as a young teenager, he might be tempted to pray. Kyle pressed the heels of his hands against his eyes. God didn't care about him, but was it possible that God cared about Ellie?

"I don't know what to do," Kyle murmured.

Harmony awoke with a start. She was a light sleeper who woke up at the slightest sound or change. The blinds in her window were open a bit, and she was surprised to find that there was light streaming through her window. She turned over and looked at the clock that sat on her bedside table. Two-thirty in the morning. Nope, not morning yet.

Harmony got up and opened her blinds so that she could see what was going on outside. Her room was at the back of the house, giving her a clear view of the patio, playground, and the outdoor skating rink. She could clearly see Kyle, lying on the ice outside with his hands pressed to his face. Harmony frowned, leaning on the window seat for a closer look. Was he hurt? Did he need help? She was relieved to see that he was moving, but what was he doing, lying on the ice in the middle of the night? Harmony debated on what to do. She could just go back to sleep or...

Harmony sighed loudly into the darkness of her room, pushing up from the window seat. She wouldn't be able to go back to sleep now anyway. Not for a while, at least. Harmony thought of her childhood in Indonesia. After her twin sister, Melody, had moved back to Canada to live with their grandparents, Harmony would wake up in the night crying for her sister. She'd been thirteen at the time, but she and Melody had done everything together, and in truth, she had felt like she'd been abandoned. Her mom would walk her down to the kitchen and make her hot chocolate loaded with whipped cream and sprinkled with chocolate shavings. Though it was an unusual treat in Indonesia, it was a little reminder of home. Her mother always told her that Melody was probably drinking hot chocolate as well, which always made Harmony feel a little more connected to her twin.

That's what she needed, she suddenly decided. Hot chocolate. It didn't matter what season; hot chocolate was an automatic pick-me-up in warm and cold weather. *Maybe Kyle could use some too,* Harmony thought to herself as she pulled on her housecoat and walked downstairs to the kitchen. She didn't have any trouble finding all the ingredients she needed; Clarissa kept a very organized kitchen.

Once Harmony had finished making the hot chocolate, she took hers and left the one for Kyle on the counter. She hoped it wouldn't be considered inappropriate to leave her boss a cup of hot chocolate in the middle of the night. She wrapped her hands around the mug as she took a big sip, breathing in the chocolaty scent as she made her way down the hallway towards the stairs.

Harmony sighed and whispered a quick prayer for this family that God had placed her in. She took another sip of hot chocolate. "God, I don't know what You have planned for me here," she said aloud, "but help me to trust that You know exactly what You're doing."

Kyle felt like slamming his hockey stick on the ice. He wouldn't have cared if he broke through one of the synthetic ice panels doing it. Skating hadn't helped at all. Usually, after a hard practice, he felt better, not worse. Aside from that, he'd been laying on the ice for about five minutes, and his shoulders were ridiculously cramped. Kyle turned off the floodlights and sat on the steps off the back porch to take off his skates. He could feel a headache starting right at the base of his skull, just another thing that was going wonderfully for him. *Yeah, everything's great,* he thought sarcastically.

As he turned to open the door, he noticed a woman exiting the kitchen. A woman with honey blond hair. "And a personality just as sweet," he muttered mockingly under his breath. What was she doing up this late anyway? Hadn't she caused enough trouble for one day? He walked into the kitchen, resisting the urge to slam the door. No sense in waking every person in the house.

Kyle glanced at the counter and nearly groaned. Harmony woke up in the middle of the night to make him hot chocolate? After everything that had happened this morning? Was she trying to make him feel like the meanest person alive? Kyle eyed the mug of hot chocolate for a minute before grabbing it and taking a long swig. Kyle closed his eyes. Man, could she make hot chocolate. Kyle sank wearily into a chair in the family room adjoining the kitchen, propping up his feet. He was asleep before he even finished his hot chocolate.

Chapter Five

"Hey, Mom, I'm going to be having some of the guys over tonight to watch the football game. We were thinking of ordering takeout or something, since it's Clarissa's night off," Kyle explained to his mother.

"Takeout? I am completely capable of cooking for you and your friends," Marjorie looked at him defiantly as though daring him to refuse her generous offer.

Kyle tried again. "Mom, you know us hockey players have such strict diets. It will be a treat to have some Chinese or pizza or something. All you'll have to do is put out some chips and things like that, okay?"

"Strict diets my foot. I've seen how you eat, Kyle Anthony Taylor. You can't fool me."

Kyle bit his tongue. She had him there. Marjorie looked like she had just swallowed a jug of vinegar, but he knew it was for the best. She had never fully recovered from her bout with cancer and the subsequent chemotherapy, and no way could she handle cooking for eight or so men with the appetites of elephants.

Harmony and Ellie came in, giggling like school girls as they skipped into the kitchen.

"Good morning everyone," Harmony greeted them cheerfully and Ellie quickly imitated her.

"Good mawning evewyone."

Kyle couldn't think for a minute or two. All he saw was Harmony, wearing simple blue jeans and a Caribbean blue T-shirt that magnified her gorgeous eyes. No woman should have the right to look that great in jeans and a T-shirt. He smiled at both of them, pushing thoughts of how great Harmony looked out and marveling at how much his daughter had changed in the few short weeks since Harmony had become her nanny. Ellie didn't creep shyly into the kitchen anymore or cower when she had to go anywhere with lots of people.

Kyle thought of Harmony's swimming lesson suggestion from a couple of days ago. In truth, he'd been able to think of little else. Watching Harmony interact with his daughter, it was obvious that she truly wanted what was best for Ellie. And that meant more to him than Harmony would ever know.

Kyle saw Marjorie press her lips into a thin line out of the corner of his eye. Kyle knew that she was not happy about him wanting to order takeout, but he sincerely hoped that she would not bring Harmony into it.

"Harmony, I have something that I need your opinion on."

Kyle groaned. Too late.

Harmony took on a wary expression close to a deer-in-the-headlights look as she glanced from Kyle to Marjorie. "My opinion on...what?"

Marjorie shot Kyle a haughty glanced that made him want to roll his eyes. Thankfully, he had a pretty good sense of self-preservation so he restrained himself. Then again, he was a hockey player, so maybe it was only self-preservation when it came to his mother.

Marjorie began her rant. "Kyle is having some of his teammates over tonight, but he refuses to let *me* cook for them. He actually suggested having takeout, so I would like your opinion."

Harmony hesitated a moment or two while she was helping Ellie get settled with her breakfast. "Well," she began, "I would imagine they probably wouldn't mind an excuse to eat some junk food, but," she brushed a strand of honey-blond hair out of her face, drawing Kyle's attention to her perfectly proportioned features, "if you want to make them something special, I would love to help you. I'm not really a very good cook, but I would like to try."

Now that might be a suitable solution, and if Harmony was helping his mother, she could make sure that Marjorie did not get overly tired. Marjorie shot him a glance and said triumphantly, "That works for me."

Kyle raised his hands in surrender. He knew when he'd been beaten. Sort of. "Okay, okay. If Harmony agrees to work with you on it, then it's fine with me." He shot Harmony a pleading glance.

She nodded and beamed at him and Marjorie. "It'll be fun."

"Can I hewp too?" asked his daughter from where she sat eating her breakfast.

Harmony nodded and smoothed Ellie's hair affectionately. "Sure thing, sweetheart."

Kyle had to look away, swallowing the lump in his throat. This arrangement was not working out well for him at all. He'd spent the last three years determined not to trust another woman and then Harmony shows up and turns his whole world upside down.

Harmony was always considerate of his mother; Abraham and Clarissa thought she was the greatest thing since sliced bread, and Ellie absolutely adored her. Here he was, trying to think of reasons why Harmony was not what she seemed, and then she did something all motherly for Ellie and...wait, *motherly*?

Kyle ran his fingers through his hair, trying to resist the urge to slam his head into the fridge. She was not, nor could she ever be Ellie's mother. What was going on with him? This nanny had him completely on edge. Why did she have to be so sweet? So caring? So pretty? *I... I mean lovable. No, no, I mean, kind.* He definitely needed some space. Now.

"Yeah, well, I, uh, will leave you ladies to it. Uh, if anyone needs me, I'll be...uh, in the office for most of the day, but I, uh, might go down to the weight room." *What is with all the uhs? Pull yourself together man.* With that, Kyle nearly sprinted from the kitchen, grabbing his protein shake on the way out.

Harmony enjoyed cooking with Marjorie and Ellie immensely. It didn't take long for her to realize that when it came to food, Marjorie didn't believe in holding back. They made hot wings, potato salad, coleslaw, deep-fried shrimp, pizza, a bunch of Kyle's favourite dishes, plus a number of elaborate desserts. Ellie mostly helped with stirring or she occupied herself with her little ball of pizza dough, babbling happily all the while. Harmony was glad to see Ellie having so much fun, and aside from the fact that she had fallen completely in love with the sweet little girl, it brought a smile to her face to see how outgoing Ellie had become.

Clarissa had gone out and bought them bags and bags of chips and bottles of pop of nearly every kind the store carried, even though she had planned to take the day off. They set up tables in the family room where the eighty-inch TV was. After all, there wasn't enough space for all the food in the theatre room. Harmony shook her head in disbelief. Sometimes it felt so wrong to be living in such luxury when she knew that so many were living in shambles.

Harmony stood back and surveyed their work. "Are you sure we didn't make too much? There's enough here to feed an army."

Marjorie laughed. "Trust me, my girl, by the end of the night, all we will have left is dirty dishes."

Harmony gazed skeptically at the mounds of food in front of them, not really believing that any group could eat that much. She would just have to trust Marjorie's superior judgment.

"Can I come too?" Ellie asked, her little hands folded prayerfully and her lip puckered out.

"It will be past your bedtime, but maybe you can stay up long enough to greet everyone," Harmony answered, squatting down to be eye level with the little girl.

Ellie's face fell, but she nodded her head mournfully. "Okay."

Harmony laughed and ruffled her hair. Marjorie offered to take Ellie for her bath and Harmony accepted graciously. When the phone rang, Harmony leapt up to get it.

"Hello?"

"Hey, is this Harmony?"

Harmony smiled. She'd recognize that voice anywhere.

"Yes, it is. I suppose this is Lucas? I figured you guys would be arriving any minute now. Are you still coming?"

He chuckled at the other side of the phone. "Yes, it's me, and yes, I'm still coming, though I'm running a few minutes late. Actually, I called because I really need to speak to Kyle. I couldn't get him on his cell phone, but I'm worried about one of the rookies and I wanted to get in touch with Kyle before we come over."

Harmony frowned in concern. "I'm not exactly sure where he is right now. Is it all right if I get him to call you back shortly? I'll be sure to give him the message right away."

Lucas sighed with relief. "Thanks, Harmony. You're the best."

Harmony hung up and hurried off to find Kyle. She made her way to the office, and finding no one, went downstairs to the exercise room. Without a second thought, she burst through the doors.

"Kyle, Lucas just called and he said—" Harmony gasped.

Kyle, who had been pumping weights when she came in, put them away and sat up watching her. And he was shirtless. Now, it wasn't as if Harmony had never seen a shirtless man. Where she had lived in Indonesia, most of the men went around shirtless almost all year long. But no one there had his body, or his good looks, his charisma, his dreamy chocolate-brown eyes...

Harmony blushed bright-red and stumbled back. "I, uh," Harmony drew a blank, completely forgetting what it was she was supposed to tell him. Hopefully it could wait. "I... I can ask you when you come upstairs."

And put a shirt on. As she backed away, she tripped over a dumbbell and felt her feet go out from under her before she hit the floor with a *thud*, practically landing on the back of her head. When she opened her eyes, Kyle was bent over her, concern melting in his captivating brown eyes and his right hand cradling her head. A shiver of awareness ran up her spine when their eyes met. Captivating eyes belonging to a captivating man. A man who was way too close for comfort. Or was it discomfort?

"Harmony, are you all right? Do you need me to get you something?"

Harmony rolled over onto her stomach and scrambled to her feet, making a quick escape to the door.

"No, I'm fine. I'm just going to go now," Harmony said without looking back.

"Wait, Harmony, what were you going to tell me?"

"I'll tell you later," Harmony called back just as she turned and slammed into the door.

Unfortunately for her, it remained closed because it opened in, not out. Harmony groaned and grabbed her forehead where she had hurt herself. *Great going, klutz. Now I hurt all over my head.* Harmony was sure that her cheeks were a bright cherry red and she wondered if she would ever survive the embarrassment.

Kyle got up and came towards her. He turned her around with a hand on her shoulder. "Here, let me help."

No way, no way, no way. "No, it's okay. I'm fine." Harmony put her free hand out to stop him, and ended up placing it directly in the center of his bare chest. Her eyes bulged wider than saucers and she jumped away from him, as if she had touched a hot stove. As she stepped back, she banged her head for the third time that afternoon. No, wait, scratch that. In the last three minutes.

Kyle looked at her quizzically but took the hint and stepped away from her, holding his arms out in surrender. "Um, Harmony, are you okay? Like, mentally stable?" The twinkle in his warm brown eyes told her he was teasing her.

Harmony still couldn't bring herself to look at him. *Oh, God, please get me out of this.* She kept her eyes steadily trained on the ground. "I, uh, Lucas called about another teammate, and, uh, he wanted you to call him back. It, um, it sounded urgent." That whole speech sounded pathetic even in her own ears. Harmony felt like she could slide through the floor, and quite happily too.

Kyle watched her with raised eyebrows. "Yeah, okay."

"Yeah, well, um, yeah, uh, bye." Harmony turned to go and Kyle reached forward and opened the door for her.

"Wouldn't want you to hurt yourself. Again."

Harmony flushed with embarrassment and made a quick escape. She would never live this down.

Kyle chuckled to himself and shook his head as he watched Harmony run away like a scared fawn. He didn't understand her. Was it something he said? Maybe he wasn't the only one feeling a bit of attraction. Oh wait, that wasn't good. Not good at all. *So, you're going to trust another woman again after what happened with Hilary?*

Wow, glad to see you've learned your lesson. You don't even really know her, Kyle thought to himself.

After a quick call to Lucas, Kyle glanced at the clock on the wall of the exercise room and realized he only had a few minutes to get ready, barely enough time to shower and clean up. Though why he wanted to clean up he had no idea—it was just a casual get together with some of the guys. And Harmony. It wasn't like he actually cared what she thought of him. Yeah, and hockey players wear tutus and figure skates. Right.

Chapter Six

Kyle entered the family room wearing a grey golf shirt and beige pants. Everyone was already there, and he noticed that Lucas and Harmony were in deep discussion. Tamping down an inexplicable surge of jealousy, he crossed the room to where some of the other guys were gathered, clapping Scott Little on the back as he approached. Scott was also a newer guy to the team, and he and Kyle had hit it off right away. Scott wasn't much younger than Kyle, probably twenty eight or so, a smaller guy at five eleven who was prematurely grey, but he was a hard worker who was always willing to listen. He didn't talk much and mostly just stayed to himself, but Kyle still considered him one of his best friends.

"Hey man, how's it going?"

Scott smiled, shaking his hand and nodding. "Can't complain. How about you?"

Kyle spoke to Scott for a while and then went on to talk to one of the other guys when his phone rang. Who would be calling him now? The game had already started, so he walked over to a quiet corner away from the TV and answered it.

"Hello?"

"Oh, hello Kyle. I hope I am not interrupting anything." Cassandra's honeyed voice reached his ears.

Cassandra had been his agent since he'd started in the NHL, but he was sure that he would never, ever understand why she was constantly putting on that fake voice whenever she talked to him. He tucked the phone between his shoulder and his ear as he grabbed a plateful of food. He was annoyed but not surprised to have Cassandra calling him; she always needed to speak to him or meet about some such nonsense that she couldn't figure out herself.

He sighed. "Just watching the football game."

"Oh well, I won't keep you long. I just wanted to make sure that we were still on for tomorrow night."

Kyle had to roll his eyes. "If I couldn't make it, I would have told you."

"Oh, well, I…" Kyle only half-listened as Cassandra droned on in his ear. He watched Harmony and Lucas out of the corner of his eye. Harmony was sitting on the arm of the sofa next to Lucas, and she laughed at something that Lucas had whispered to her. Kyle felt the cold hand of jealousy creeping around his heart. He didn't even have a right, nor did he have a want, to be jealous anyway. "Kyle? Are you listening to me?"

"What? Yeah, yeah, of course. Just—" Kyle didn't get a chance to finish his sentence because at that moment, he heard the door burst opened and saw his sister, Lily, run into the family room and make a beeline for his mother. A hundred questions burst into his mind at the sight of her. What was his sister doing here? Why wasn't she in Toronto? And why was she crying? Kyle knew that he should be worried. Lily *never* cried. Ever. "Hey, listen Cassandra, I've got to go. I've got a situation."

"Does this situation happen to concern a young nanny?" Cassandra's malicious voice rang void as he hung up the phone. Every eye in the room was trained on Kyle. "I'll be back in a minute," he muttered, grasping at straws. He heard Harmony's voice as he left the room, asking if anyone else needed a drink. *Thank you, Harmony.* First things first: go help his little sister. Kyle walked out of the room to follow his mother and sister, the sister he hadn't seen cry since the day they found out that their father had died.

Cassandra put down the phone and stared angrily out of her apartment window. She knew that Kyle had hired a new nanny, without consulting her first, and she knew from this Harmony Clark's resumé that she was young, single, and definitely available. She was a threat. Not only that, but the woman was living with Kyle. Her Kyle. Cassandra blinked back angry tears. She was already thirty-three and still, here she was, single and not even dating anyone. Cassandra knew that Kyle was the man of her dreams and she was certain she would be the perfect Mrs. Taylor. She had been Kyle's agent for his entire professional career and she had worked too hard, flirting, calculating, and scheming to have it all taken away by some wet-behind-the-ears young nanny who obviously thought she would be the perfect addition to the Taylor family.

"Well, I'll just have to fix that," Cassandra said into the emptiness of her apartment. And fix it she would.

Kyle made his way to his office where his mother had undoubtedly taken his sister. As he entered the room, Marjorie was desperately trying to soothe his now hysterical sister. He clenched his hands into fists. He couldn't stand seeing his sister all riled up like this. "Mom, what's going on?"

"I don't really know, Kyle. She's only said she's been driving for the past two days to get here."

Kyle squeezed the back of his neck and looked uncomfortably at his mother and sister. Emotional scenes were really not his forte. "Come on, Lily. It can't be that bad. Knock it off and tell us what's happened," he said awkwardly, nudging her shoulder with his hand.

Lily visibly tried to pull herself together, taking a shuddering breath before speaking. "He used me and took it all," she hiccuped, "my savings, my business, everything." She ended on a wail.

"Do you mean Howard?" Marjorie asked with concern, shooting a worried glance in Kyle's direction. Lily owned a successful spa business in Toronto. Kyle couldn't understand how it was possible for her to lose it. She'd never wanted to do anything else.

Lily nodded silently as a fresh bout of tears filled her eyes and ran down her cheeks.

"I knew that guy was a jerk right from the beginning!" Kyle burst out angrily, though he wasn't angry at her but rather at the two-faced Howard who he had never liked.

"Yeah, well, it's not like you're the best judge of character!" Lily shot back, though by the look in her eyes, she regretted it instantly. "I... I'm sorry, just the emotion talking. I didn't mean that, really. But it doesn't matter. I got sucked in, and now I've got nothing. I'm sorry, I... I had nowhere else to go," Lily said in obvious embarrassment and remorse.

"Of course, you had to come here, dear, and you always have us," Marjorie said comfortingly.

"Don't worry about it, Lily. You are welcome here for as long as you want. I'll get my lawyer to help you and we'll get it all back," Kyle said, laying a hand on her shoulder.

"I don't want to sue him. I don't want to see him ever again. I was stupid and got what I deserved and now I just want to be rid of him. I w-was having financial trouble and he o-offered to help. He convinced me to put his name on everything."

"If you needed help, why didn't you just ask? You know I would always help you," Kyle said. He was still a little hurt by her previous comment and even more so by the fact that she'd gone to her low life boyfriend instead of him for help.

"I don't want to have to ask you for money all the time. It makes me feel like I'm using you," Lily explained.

"Well, get over it. I'll find you a new site here, and you can rename everything and start again." Lily started to protest, but Kyle held up his hand to silence her. "Listen, Lil. I'm helping and you're not stopping me. End of discussion."

It probably would not have been the end of the discussion if someone had not gently rapped on the office door. Harmony and Ellie peaked in through the door.

"I'm sorry to bother you, Marjorie, Kyle, but it's time for Ellie to go to bed and she wanted to kiss you both goodnight."

When Ellie spotted Lily, she bolted across the room and launched herself into her lap. "Auntie," she cried excitedly, "you're here. Do you want to come pway wit me?"

"Sweetie, I can hardly wait to play with you, but we have to wait until tomorrow because it's your bedtime and Auntie is really tired, okay?" Lily said, hugging the little girl as she wiped away the remainder of her tears.

"Okay, Auntie, but I can hardwy wait! Come on, Miss Hawmony. We got to go to bed so I can get up soon to pway wit Auntie." The little girl got up from the couch and reached for Harmony's hand, trying to pull her towards the doorway, completely forgetting the reason they had come in the first place.

"Harmony, this is my daughter, Lily. She will be staying with us for a while." Marjorie introduced them, then bent down, holding her arms out for a hug from her granddaughter.

"Hi, Lily. It's nice to meet you," Harmony said pleasantly.

"Yes, you too," Lily replied a little warily. Kyle wondered what was going on inside her head. What was she thinking? In retrospect, Harmony's sugary sweet personality was a little disarming. Kyle glanced at Harmony out of the corner of his eye. It was hard to believe that anyone could be that...perfect.

"Kyle, why don't you and Harmony put Ellie to bed and then get back to your guests? They must be wondering what's happened. I'll take care of getting Lily settled and then head to bed myself. I'm a little tuckered out too."

"Okay, Mom. Sleep in tomorrow and rest up please. Good night, Lily. Sleep well," Kyle said, leaning over to kiss both his Mom and sister on their cheeks. He picked Ellie up and said, "Come on, kiddo. It's bedtime for you." Kyle noticed Ellie's eyes widen as he picked her up. She stiffened and glanced at Harmony. Harmony smiled encouragingly at her and smoothed her hair out of her face before Ellie finally relaxed in his arms. Was he really so much of a stranger to her? Talk about dad of the year.

Kyle gritted his teeth. Harmony was right: He needed to spend more time with his daughter. Quality time. No way did he want to be one of those dads who saw their kid at meals and for an hour in the evening while the nanny raised them. Kyle felt like everything in his "perfect" world was tumbling down. He glanced at Harmony out of the corner of his eye. And it all started when "the nanny" arrived. It was strange how much Harmony was changing their lives. Now, his life had never been great, but it also hadn't been horrible. Ever since the Hilary debacle, his life had been comfortable, mundane, safe. Nothing risky.

While they were putting Ellie to bed, she asked something that Kyle never thought he would hear.

"Can you wead me a bible stowy?" Ellie asked, pulling the covers up around her ears. Harmony beamed at Ellie and hurried to grab the old children's Bible, which was not surprisingly pink. Afterwards, they prayed with Ellie—a thing he had never done before—then went their separate ways, with Harmony stopping him for a minute to ask about Lily. As Kyle went back downstairs to hang out with the guys, he couldn't help feeling that this was how it should always be.

Chapter Seven

The next morning after breakfast, Harmony was sitting with Ellie, reading her devotion while the little girl coloured with Clarissa at the far side of the room. Lily had come down to join them, and Marjorie chose to go take a little siesta after her morning meal. Lily hadn't said much, but Harmony could feel her watching her out of the corner of her eye, as if sizing her up.

"So, Harmony, how long have you been working here?" Harmony glanced up in surprise at the question.

"Almost a month now."

Lily nodded suspiciously. "Huh. What made you decide to become Ellie's nanny?"

"Well," Harmony grinned when she thought about it, "I thought I'd be helping a family in need."

Lily raised her perfectly arched eyebrows. "Seriously? What, you'd never heard of Kyle Taylor?" she asked disbelievingly.

Harmony shook her head sheepishly. Kyle Taylor was a very well-known hockey player after all. Granted, he was much more famous in Ottawa, and she'd only just come back to Canada, but it still seemed silly that she hadn't at least heard about Kyle Taylor. Anyone with a TV knew who he was.

"Where did you grow up, under a rock?"

Harmony smiled, not at all offended by the question. "Pretty close to it. My parents were missionaries. Well, they still are, in a remote village in Indonesia. I lived there for most of my life."

"Wow, that must have been really interesting," Lily stated excitedly, her cold demeanor fading. "I never would have guessed it. You look like a normal Canadian girl to me. Why did you come back?"

A lump rose in the back of Harmony's throat. She was struck by the desire to have someone to talk to, to vent to, to confide in, but…she didn't think she was ready for that yet. She took a steadying breath before answering.

"I came back after my fiancé died." Harmony really did not want to elaborate. Lily's eyes were warm and compassionate. Harmony didn't want compassion. She wanted Roger.

"Oh, Harmony. I'm so sorry. I didn't know."

Kyle chose that moment to enter the kitchen and Harmony blinked back tears, grateful for the interruption.

"Morning, ladies," Kyle greeted them before directing his attention to Harmony. "Harmony, I was wondering if you would like to start Ellie's swimming lessons today, since I don't have hockey practice."

"Oh, sure. I can manage that," Harmony answered eagerly. She felt that if she taught Ellie to swim, she would be honoring Roger's memory, considering the horrific way he died. Not that she wanted to dwell on that. "I can get her ready right now if you want," Harmony added.

Kyle smiled and nodded. "Sure thing. I'll meet you guys at the pool."

Lily frowned. "But we were getting along so well," she feigned a whine. Lily glanced at Kyle. "You have to share her."

"Don't worry. We can talk later," Harmony hastened to say.

As she left the room with Ellie, she heard Lily say rather mournfully, "Okay, talk to ya later."

*****

Harmony stood in the shallow end of the pool, gently trying to coax Ellie into the water. "Come on, Ellie. It's really nice in here, and we'll have lots of fun with your daddy." Ellie glanced at her curiously.

"Daddy coming?"

Harmony nodded. "Yes, your daddy loves you so much and he wants to make sure that you're always safe, so he's going to help teach you to swim. You'll like that, right?" Harmony smiled at her, holding her breath. After the way Ellie had reacted to asking her dad about going to the water park, she wasn't sure how Ellie would feel about swimming with her dad, but she felt the need to act as a bridge between Ellie and Kyle. Besides, Kyle was obviously reaching out to his daughter, and Harmony was not going to make that any more difficult than it had to be.

Ellie cocked her head to one side, considering Harmony's words. "Okay." Ellie dipped her feet into the water, held out her arms, and let Harmony pull her into the water. Ellie quickly got used to being in the pool, and she was quite content to sit on Harmony's lap and splash in the water.

While they were waiting for Kyle, the pool doors opened and a tall, platinum blonde with flashy jewelry and ridiculously high heels waltzed into the room. The woman stopped and glared at Harmony. "Who are you? What are you even doing here?" The woman obviously didn't expect an answer because she continued without even taking a breath. "Where's Kyle?"

Harmony didn't speak. She was confused enough as it was about this strange woman who seemed to believe she owned the place

The woman rolled her eyes. "I so don't have time for this." She turned to Ellie who was now clinging to Harmony with all her might. "Come on, kid, tell her who I am." Ellie stared wide-eyed at the imposing woman.

"I no know you."

The woman's mouth dropped open. "Why, you lying little—"

"Hey!" Harmony's cheeks flushed with anger and her voice cut into the woman's angry tirade. "That is not the way you speak to a child."

The woman looked as if she was about to start another diatribe, but thankfully, Kyle chose that moment to enter the pool deck and Harmony waded away from the angry woman before she had the chance to say something she might regret.

"What are you doing here, Cassandra?"

Kyle had entered the pool deck just in time to hear Harmony giving Cassandra what for. Harmony's voice had been low and steady, but her voice left no room for argument. Her eyes were fixed on Cassandra, her chin set with a defiant determination that he hadn't expected from quiet, meek Harmony. Kyle shot a sidelong glance at Cassandra, wondering what had inspired the fierce protectiveness in Harmony.

Cassandra stopped as if she had been shot, ran a hand through her hair, and turned to him with a smile so fake it almost made him sick.

"Kyle! Who's my favourite client?" She came up to him and gave him a hug. "How have you been?"

Kyle stepped away from her and gave her a tight smile. Out of the corner of his eye, he could see Harmony cradling Ellie and whispering softly to her. What exactly had happened in here?

"Hey, Cassandra. What was going on a minute ago when I came in? You sounded angry."

Cassandra smiled a sickly sweet smile and laughed. "Oh no, I was just a bit frustrated. We had a little misunderstanding and no one seemed to know where you were." She motioned towards Harmony and Ellie. "Are you going to introduce me to your...friend?"

He hated her tone. What did it matter to her who he spent his time with? "This is Harmony Clark, my daughter's nanny."

"Oh well, that's wonderful, really, but what I came to talk to you about was another contract for you. Do you have a minute?"

Kyle had known Cassandra long enough to know that a minute would soon turn into an hour. "I'm busy right now. I'll call you later."

Cassandra frowned and shot Harmony the dirtiest look he had ever seen. Then she flipped her hair over her shoulder and sauntered towards the door. "Well, I really only came by to make sure we were still on for tonight."

He nodded and rolled his eyes, glad to watch her head out the door. They needed to go over some of his new endorsement contracts, and Cassandra had suggested going for dinner instead of meeting at his office. He didn't understand why she would need to check and double-check the fact that yes, they were still on for tonight. It was just business. He made his way towards Harmony who was holding a much calmer Ellie at the side of the pool. Was it all as simple as

Cassandra claimed it had been? Or had something else happened? He still wasn't sure, but at least Ellie didn't look too traumatized. "Hey, Ellie, are you okay?" Kyle asked softly.

Harmony glanced up at him. "I think she's fine, just a little shaken." Then she whispered something to Ellie and the little girl perked up.

"Can we go swimming now?"

He smiled and kissed her forehead. "Sure thing, sweetheart."

As they waded about in the shallow end, Kyle was annoyed to find that Ellie refused to do *anything* without Harmony.

"Wow," he muttered. "My own daughter prefers the nanny over me."

Harmony heard him and looked at him apologetically. "It's only because I've been spending so much time with her."

Great, Kyle thought to himself, *another reminder as to how little time I spend with my daughter.* "Here, Ellie. Let me teach you how to float." Kyle reached for her, but she clutched Harmony and shook her head wildly. "Come on, Ellie," Kyle said, aggravated. But she refused to calm down, and finally, he said, "Fine. Miss Harmony will float with you the first time."

Harmony's eyes widened and she shook her head. "Kyle," she whispered, "I don't think that's such a good idea."

He looked at her and rolled his eyes. "Knock it off, Harmony. You're freaking Ellie out."

No, no, no. This could not be happening. Let him *hold* her? But she could tell that he was adamant that she help Ellie. Harmony supposed it would be for the best. Maybe, if she showed Ellie how easy it was, she would do it alone.

"Well...okay." She relented. "Don't worry, Ellie. It'll be fun," she said, forcing fake cheerfulness into her voice.

She held Ellie against her and Kyle lowered them into the water. Thank goodness he had decided to wear a T-shirt. He had one hand on the small of her back and the other hand under her head. Tingles ran up and down her spine and she almost shivered. How did she get into this predicament? She looked up at him, and for a moment, their eyes locked and he blushed. He actually *blushed.*

He quickly put both her and Ellie back on their feet. "See, Ellie? It's easy." Kyle refused to look into her eyes.

Ellie glanced at Harmony, and when she nodded her head, Ellie waved her arms and smiled. "Me next, me next!" she squealed.

Harmony smiled and waded over to the side of the pool. Ellie and Kyle were now splashing and playing about in the water, looking for all the world as if they had not seen each other in years. Maybe they hadn't. Harmony felt as if she were intruding on a private conversation, but she couldn't tear herself away. Every time she tried to, Kyle would look up at her and tell her that she didn't need to go. So she didn't. And she grew more and more aware that with every passing moment, this little family was burrowing its way deeper into her heart.

Chapter Eight

Later, once they were all dried and dressed from their swim, Kyle couldn't believe how much fun he had. Why hadn't he ever thought of this before? Harmony was right. By not spending time with Ellie, he was missing out, and worse, he was making Ellie miss out too. He stopped Harmony on her way out and told her so.

"You're right," he whispered. "I should be spending more time with Ellie."

She turned around and smiled at him, such a dazzling smile that made him catch his breath. She was gorgeous.

"I'm so happy to hear that, Kyle. Thank you for telling me."

As Kyle watched her and Ellie go upstairs for lunch, he realized he had a big problem. He was definitely falling for Harmony. Hard. Yeah, that really wasn't good. Kyle ran his fingers through his hair. He couldn't be falling in love with his daughter's nanny. Kyle mentally shook himself. That was ridiculous. Besides, he'd known her for just over a month. People didn't really fall in love that fast, did they?

He glanced at his watch, pushing thoughts of Harmony out of his mind and dwelling instead on his business meeting with Cassandra. Maybe he should go up to his office and do some work. And then he would have to look into commercial properties available for Lily to use to restart her spa business thing. He sighed. So much to do with so little time. Even so, he would not have traded the last few hours he spent with Harmony and Ellie for the world.

Kyle went up to his office, finished some paperwork, looked up some nice big buildings for his sister, made an appointment with his realtor in order to tour the buildings, and even managed to get ready to meet Cassandra in time. He made his way down to the kitchen and addressed his mother who was there with Harmony, Lily, Ellie, and Clarissa.

"Hey, Mom. I'm just going out to the Steak House with Cassandra tonight. You know, business stuff," he added hurriedly. His mother was not a big fan of Cassandra, so he meant to dispel any inclination of a romantic relationship between him and Cassandra. Kyle shuddered at the thought.

"Oh...really?" Marjorie said in a short, almost offended voice. "And when might you be back?"

"Around nine at the latest. It really shouldn't take that long, but if you need me, you can call my cell." He leaned over and gave her a kiss on the cheek. "Love you, Mom. Bye, guys."

Ellie raised her head and asked, "Daddy, gotta go?"

Kyle scooped her up and gave her a kiss on the forehead. "I'll be back soon, sweetheart," he whispered before handing her back to Harmony.

Their gazes locked for a split second before she looked away. That one look nearly took his breath away. A man could get lost in those eyes, a mixture of different shades of blue overflowing with compassion and kindness. Yet there was a sadness to them, and Kyle had the deepest desire to know what had put that sadness there and to be the one to put joy back into her expressive blue eyes.

Taken aback by the depth of his feelings, Kyle stepped back and darted out of the kitchen, towards the front door, and down the drive to where he had parked his flashy red sports car. Kyle had two cars, this one and a silver SUV, though the SUV was usually driven by his mom or Harmony. Kyle had bought the red and silver cars intentionally, because his team's colours were red, silver, and black. When he got to the steak house, he met Cassandra at a cozy table for two, tucked away at the back of the restaurant. It seemed inconvenient to Kyle to be sitting so far away from the doors. It wasn't like they needed the privacy; Kyle wasn't as well-known in Calgary as he'd been in Ottawa after all.

Kyle and Cassandra had been discussing endorsement contract for a while after supper when Cassandra got a bit off track.

"So, Kyle," she began, "how long have you known this new nanny?"

Kyle sat back in his chair. He just had to grin as he said, "Since she moved in with me."

Kyle nearly laughed when Cassandra choked and sputtered on her Chardonnay. He honestly couldn't see why she would care. When she finally recovered, she asked again.

"No, Kyle. Seriously, how long have you known this woman?"

"I was being serious," he shot back lazily.

"Okay, okay, whatever. I just want you to be careful. This girl has 'manipulative' written all over her." Kyle didn't even bother to try not to roll his eyes at that statement. Harmony was the nicest, sweetest, kindest, prettiest, most beautiful woman...*Okay, wow,* he mentally shook himself. *Where exactly did I leave my brain?*

"Nah, I don't think so. Harmony's like, sweet enough to make your tooth ache."

Cassandra looked at Kyle beseechingly and sighed. She reached forward and grabbed his hand. "Kyle, I say this because I care about your well-being. I mean, think about it. A single young woman coming all the way from Indonesia to come and be nanny to *your* daughter. *You,* one of the most eligible and sought-after NHL players in the country. You never know if someone has, well, ulterior motives."

Kyle raised an eyebrow and pulled his hand out of her grasp. "And what might those 'ulterior motives' be?" he asked, not quite believing that Harmony could even try to think like that, but he was intrigued nonetheless.

"Well, you know," Cassandra began, warming up as she went along. "You might find her in your room, or maybe your office, looking for something to sell online, and besides, you did say that her parents were missionaries. She might be trying to weasel some money out of you. Or she could be from one of the local newspapers, even one of the global ones, looking for dirt on the marvelous Kyle Taylor. Don't forget. You may be famous, but you don't have as many local fans as you used to, considering you were only just traded from Ottawa. Oh, she won't do it outright. She'll pump up your ego, feed you a sob story, or even stoop to trying to get you infatuated with her. Also, being your daughter's nanny, she has every opportunity to get that precious little girl wrapped around her little finger, getting her to turn on you and do her dirty work. Even if she gets caught red-handed, she'll have a ready excuse. Trust me. I've seen her type before."

Cassandra paused for a minute, no doubt for dramatic effect, and Kyle had to keep himself from yawning. The stuff Cassandra came up with. She could make movies with an imagination like that.

"The fact is, you don't know her very well, and you really do have no idea what she is capable of." Cassandra finished with a dramatic sigh and looked him dead in the eye. "If I were you, I would be very, very careful. You have been fooled by a blond before," she said, almost sneering.

Kyle immediately bristled. It was bad enough that Cassandra was ranting about conspiracy and ulterior motive when they were supposed to be having a business meeting. She'd practically dug her own grave with the blond comment.

"In case you forgot," Kyle stated coolly, "you're a blond too." He had pronounced each syllable with extra emphasis just to get the point across. A horrified, insulted look crossed Cassandra's face just as the waiter came over with the bill. Kyle paid as Cassandra composed herself and put on an apologetic smile.

"Oh, Kyle, I never meant to bring back bad memories. I am sorry. I guess we should be going, but..." Cassandra left the invitation in the air, but Kyle refused to fall for the bait.

"Listen, I've got to go. I'll see you next time."

On his way home, Kyle thought about what Cassandra had said. No, he wouldn't let it bother him. And not just because she'd sounded like some crazy conspiracy theorist, but because Harmony had never given him a reason to distrust her. Cassandra's overactive imagination would not change that. Though in truth, being cautious never hurt anybody, and while he wouldn't change his opinion of Harmony, just in case, knowing was always half the battle.

Chapter Nine

Harmony had been playing with Ellie and Mookie from after supper till bedtime, but all the while, she couldn't silence her very vocal conscience. What on earth did she think she was doing? Swimming with Kyle and Ellie had made it more than apparent, and the way her heart leapt at the very mention of Kyle's name was a serious cause of concern. Harmony definitely had feelings for him.

Harmony sighed as she tucked Ellie in and listened to her prayers. She thought she would be doing something good teaching a young girl to swim, something that Roger would have wanted. But now she wasn't so sure. *How could you?* her conscience accused. *You are falling for your boss, forgetting all about Roger. About how much you loved him. About how it's your fault that he's gone. You killed him!*

I haven't forgotten, Harmony argued with herself. *Roger was my everything, the love of my life.* Harmony shook her head, trying to stop the argument going on in her mind. *Even if I did...care for Kyle, I don't deserve to move on. Not after what I did.* She and Kyle weren't meant to be, and she just had to keep reminding herself of that.

Ellie was now snuggled down beneath her quilts and Harmony sat on the comfy window seat with pink cushions at the end of the room. Usually, after tucking Ellie in, she sat in the kitchen and visited with Marjorie or Clarissa for a while. Tonight, Clarissa had gone home early, Marjorie was at a ladies' bible study and Lily had gone along with her. Harmony knew Ellie didn't need her anymore, but she just couldn't bring herself to leave. She tried to pray, but guilt over Roger's death crowded out all other thoughts.

Oh, Roger, Harmony drew in a shuddering breath, a lump forming in her throat. *I'm so sorry for letting you down.* "Dear God," Harmony prayed before she fell asleep, "forgive me..."

When Harmony opened her eyes, she was back in the pool with Ellie when suddenly, Ellie slipped from her arms and disappeared under the water. When Harmony pulled her up again, it wasn't Ellie. It was Roger and he was gasping, coughing, feverish in her arms.

"Roger!" she screamed. "No, don't leave me. Please don't leave me." Tears were running down her face. Something pulled them apart and Roger turned his face away from her. When he turned back, he was Kyle. "Kyle, no, not you too. Please." A new sense of panic seized Harmony as she pleaded with him, begging him not to die, not to leave her. She could feel the life leaving him as if all the oxygen in the atmosphere was being sucked away. Horrified, she reached for him, but he was too far away. Was this God's way of punishing her? She wasn't what she should have been to Roger, so Kyle had to die too? Growing frantic, Harmony called his name. "Kyle!"

Kyle arrived home to a dark house. It seemed unlikely to think that everyone was already asleep; typically, the adults stayed up talking.

Kyle shrugged to himself, dismissing the thought, and as he made his way up to his room, he decided to check on Ellie before he went to sleep. He entered Ellie's room and went over to where his little princess was sleeping. Ellie lay snuggled beneath the covers, and a giant pink stuffed bunny lay at her side. Kyle smiled and leaned forward to kiss her forehead.

Just before he left, he heard a sound from the edge of the room. It almost sounded like a sob. He turned around and saw Harmony hunched up in the corner of the window seat, crying silently. The soft moonlight streaming in through the window cast her in a silvery glow, magnifying the look of her tears. She looked like she was sleeping, but she was moaning and fidgeting quietly, and every few seconds, she reached forward and grabbed at one of the pillows across from her, only skimming the fabric. She was saying someone's name, something like "Robert" or "Roger." He even thought he heard his name called. Kyle debated on whether or not to wake her. He sighed. He couldn't just leave her there. Kyle closed the distance between himself and Harmony and then he bent to wake her.

"Harmony," he whispered quietly, shaking her gently. "Harmony, wake up." She woke with a start and looked around the room frantically before throwing herself into his arms.

"Kyle, you're all right." With that she broke down and sobbed against his shoulder, muffling the sound enough not to wake Ellie. It was all he could do to console her. He knew he shouldn't be there holding her, even though it wasn't under romantic circumstances, but…he just couldn't let her go. Having her wrapped in his arms and holding her while she cried just felt so…right. Like she was meant to be there. Which she was not. Kyle gently tried to untangle himself in order to get a little more breathing room and maybe clear his head. More like get Harmony out of it.

"Come on, Harmony. It can't be as bad as that," he murmured quietly, painfully aware of how beautiful she looked, even with a red nose and tears running down her face. "Come downstairs with me and I'll make you a hot chocolate. It won't be as good as yours but I'll do my best."

She looked up surprised and seemed to forget her anguish for a moment. "How do you know I can make hot chocolate?"

Kyle grinned a laid-back, easy grin that he hoped would ease her. "You're the one who left hot chocolate for me the other night, weren't you?" Harmony blushed so red that he could see her complexion change even in the dark room.

"I-It could have been Marjorie, or, or even Clarissa," she stuttered and spoke quickly, as if it was some major crime to make hot chocolate for him. Why would she think that?

"You're right," Kyle nodded slowly. "I might have believed that except for the fact that I saw you."

"Oh" was all she said to that. He led her downstairs and into the kitchen where he began making her some hot chocolate. It really was no comparison to her hot chocolate, but it would have to do. He turned towards her and gave her the hot chocolate knowing full well that she was not going to like the question that he was going to ask, but the truth was, he needed answers.

Harmony gingerly sipped her cup of hot chocolate. She could not believe that she had literally thrown herself into her boss's arms.

How could she have? And what a silly nightmare! It hadn't even made sense, yet it had been so vivid that she had actually believed that it was real. Kyle turned towards her and leaned his forearms on the table, exposing his muscular arms beneath his button-down dress shirt.

"So, what's up?" he asked, his brown eyes warm and compassionate.

"I, I'm sorry, I, well, I was having a nightmare." Harmony felt stupid saying it out loud.

Kyle shook his head, his eyes never leaving hers. "That's not what I meant," he said, and the look he gave her told her exactly what he meant.

Harmony met his gaze and was once again reminded of what a wonderful man he was. Someday, he would make some lucky woman very happy. But that woman would not be her. *And just you remember that,* Harmony reminded herself. Kyle hadn't even bothered to pour himself a cup of hot chocolate. When she looked in his eyes, all she saw was concern. Compassion. For her.

"What were you dreaming about?" Kyle spoke in a quiet, gentle voice, almost a whisper.

"My fiancé," Harmony choked out. "He died a year ago in the mission field in a…a flash flood." Harmony closed her eyes, trying not to cry as the memories of that day came back to her as fast as the flash flood that had killed her fiancé.

It had started off as a nice day. It was a bit cloudy, but it didn't look like it was going to rain, so the clouds were no cause for worry. Harmony was preparing picnic tables for that afternoon. She and the other missionaries at the "camp" were going to be holding a service and a potluck lunch afterwards. Harmony was in charge of taking care of the kids and keeping them entertained with games and bible stories while the adults had bible study and helped with the potluck.

Over the course of maybe two or three hours, the sky darkened and it began to rain. The wind picked up and scattered the food, picnic cloths, and all sorts of things. The river, which had already been up past its banks, was like a torrent of death, swirling and rolling, the current dragging anything that touched the water down to its depths. Harmony looked over to where Roger, her fiancé, was standing, and their gazes locked. Both of them had been serving here long enough to know that a flash flood might be in the cards. They had ushered everyone up to higher ground when a high pitched scream cut through the air.

Harmony turned towards the river and felt her heart drop into her stomach. On a high rock, half-submerged in the water, was a small girl, probably about seven-years-old, crying and clinging to the rock for dear life. Suddenly, everyone panicked. The little girl's parents were rushing down and trying to get to her, only to be stopped by other villagers because of the dangerous swells. Roger ran up to where Harmony was with the other children and gave her his coat.

"I've got to go get her."

Harmony couldn't believe her ears. "Are you crazy?!" She had to scream in order to be heard above the wind and rain. "You can't go down there. It's too dangerous."

"I have to try!" he shouted back. Roger turned around and ran down the hill towards the water.

"Roger! Roger!" Harmony ran down the hill after him. He couldn't leave. He wouldn't make it. Roger stopped abruptly and turned around. "Roger, please." Harmony couldn't let him leave. Roger pulled her into his arms and kissed her.

"I love you," he whispered against her skin, before diving into the overflow towards the girl. He reached her and had to practically yank her from the rocks in order to save her before he could try and swim back to shore. Harmony was sure she would die when she saw them both go under. After what seemed like an eternity, they finally resurfaced and were dragged up the rest of the way to shore by some of the strong village men. The little girl was taken away by her parents. Two days later Roger was sick with a lung infection. Harmony sat with him every day, never leaving his side. He was delirious with fever half the time and coughing up mucus the other half. He survived for another half a day before he succumbed to his illness. He died in Harmony's arms. She could feel the life leaving him as he breathed his last, not even knowing who she was. She was begging him not to go. Not to leave her.

"Just hold on a little bit longer. For me, Roger. For me!" Harmony's desperate pleas and prayers seemed to fall on deaf ears. Her parents came *and gently guided her away from her fiancé's lifeless body, which had once held the nicest, most caring, and loving spirit, so on fire for God and his people, wanting to go to the ends of the earth so that the whole world would know. And now he was gone. And it was all her fault.*

Harmony tried to keep control over the feelings assaulting her mind. Her heart. Her soul. She was responsible for her fiancé's death. She'd been in charge of taking care of the children at the mission. If she'd been doing her job, that little girl would not have been out in middle of that flash flood. And Roger would not have died.

God, she prayed, *Oh, Lord, I need you. Help me cope.* She couldn't possibly tell Kyle. She was not going to break down crying in front of her boss. At least not again.

"Harmony—"

"Cinnamon." Harmony interrupted him. Kyle looked at her quizzically. Harmony took a deep breath. She was stalling, not wanting to dig up the pass.

"The secret to my hot chocolate is melted milk chocolate and a hint of cinnamon."

Kyle started to say something else but Harmony cut him off.

"Listen, Kyle, I… I am really sorry for, for disturbing you, but I really don't think I want to talk about it right now. Besides, it's late and I should go to bed. Got to wake up bright and early tomorrow." Harmony tried to add some cheerfulness into her voice. As though it was just a silly nightmare and that she was fine. That she was over it. But the sad truth was that she wasn't sure she would ever recover, ever heal, or ever forget. Ever.

Kyle sat down in the now-empty kitchen, bewildered and curious, wondering what could have happened that made Harmony react like she had. Kyle wished that she would only trust him, that she would let him be the one to take away her pain and her sorrow. Just to see her smile again. She'd looked so sad, so alone. Maybe that was the reason for the sadness that lurked in her deep blue eyes.

Kyle had a nagging thought at the back of his mind, one which he refused to dwell on. *She'll no doubt feed you some sob story.* But she hadn't. Harmony wouldn't. So she'd awakened from a nightmare crying and had basically thrown herself into his arms. Not that he minded. Yet the nagging remained and he could practically hear Cassandra's mocking voice, saying, "You think those tears were real? This type of person is a born actress, and she will have no problem winding you up and then stamping you down when you are no longer needed." Kyle groaned. It was enough that Cassandra was his agent; he didn't have to start thinking like her. Besides, Harmony wasn't like that, and she would never do anything like that to him or anyone else for that matter.

Right?

Chapter Ten

"Whoa, wait a second. What?"

Marjorie sighed and put down her knitting. "I told the pastor of our church that it would be fine if he held the weekly adults' bible study here. You do remember telling me when I moved here that I could make myself right at home, don't you? My house is your house right? So I told him it would be fine. That's not a problem is it?"

Kyle sighed and rubbed the bridge of his nose. He hated it when his mother did that, using what he said against him to beat him into a corner. *Smooth, Mom.* "Fine, whatever, but don't expect me to show up." Kyle turned around to leave when Marjorie called him.

"Kyle, honey," she said soothingly, "you don't have to be afraid to trust God with your future. I know you feel like you've been handed some tough breaks lately, but really, we have been so blessed, considering what other people are going through."

Kyle sighed. Yes, he had it a lot better than most people, but was he blessed? Apparently, that was a matter of opinion.

"Mom, you say that Jesus saved your life or something, but if you ask me, when you became a Christian, that's when all of our problems started. Me going to your bible study probably wouldn't help either of us."

Marjorie smiled. "Honey, did you ever try reading the Bible? God's word is a letter to you filled with promises and advice for everything in life. Proverbs 3:5–6 says: 'Trust in the Lord with all thine heart; and lean not unto thine own understanding. In all thy ways acknowledge him, and he shall direct thy paths.' All you have to do is trust in the Lord." Marjorie was watching him with hope, thinking she might have just converted him.

Kyle almost felt bad. Almost. At the same time, all the cons were flying through his mind. Had he ever read his Bible? He'd tried a few times, but when was he supposed to fit it into his schedule between work, Ellie, and his mother? And besides, Marjorie was constantly preaching at him, telling him to get his life right with the Lord. Yeah, every time he tried that, something bad happened. Mom and Dad got a divorce. Dad died. He met Hilary. Mom got cancer. Ellie was born.

Kyle stopped himself. Ellie was the best thing that ever happened to him. She was the highlight of his life. That and her new nanny.

Whoa, whoa, hold it. Get back on track here. Remind me. Why can't God be trusted? Because Lily's boyfriend used her. Because in a world with this much wrong, how could there be such a "good" God? What if God was just as bad as the rest of us? What if He didn't exist at all? It didn't matter who was selling, his mom, Harmony, or anyone else. Kyle Anthony Taylor was not buying.

"Listen, Mom, when God starts writing his letters in regular English, I might try reading one." Or he might not. Marjorie picked up her knitting and didn't even try to hide the motherly smirk on her face as she said, "God works in mysterious ways."

When Kyle entered the hallway, the first thing he saw was Harmony. With Lucas. And they were totally flirting. Argh. Could this day get any worse?

Lucas glanced up and saw him as he made his way down the hallway. Lucas gave him a smirk and turned back to Harmony.

"Wow, Harmony, it's awesome that Marjorie offered to host the bible study here," Kyle heard Lucas saying. "Thank you so much for inviting me. I'd love to come."

Kyle frowned. Figures that Lucas would be thrilled to come here for bible study.

"Hey, guys," Kyle said nonchalantly. *Breathe, Taylor. Don't lose your head,* Kyle silently coached himself. "Hope I'm not interrupting something."

"Harmony was just telling me that you'd be hosting bible study here. Good for you, Kyle, getting on board," Lucas was practically gushing. What on earth was wrong with him? Was Lucas really making such a fuss over bible study?

"Whoa, just because my mom's hosting it here doesn't mean I'm going," Kyle grumbled, narrowing his eyes at Lucas.

"Oh well, I will definitely be there." Lucas gave Harmony a megawatt smile. Kyle couldn't help the feeling that Lucas was messing with him, trying to egg him on.

Relax, Taylor. It's not a big deal. You're fine—

"That's great, Lucas," Harmony said happily. "I will look forward to seeing you."

Kyle shot a look at Harmony. *Oh yay, we get to see Lucas,* Kyle thought sarcastically.

"Harmony, where is Ellie? I'm pretty sure I pay you to take care of her, not my guests."

Harmony recoiled as if she'd been struck and stared at him a moment, her lips pursed into the shape of an *O*. She mumbled something about having to go check on Ellie before darting up the stairs. Kyle turned to go when Lucas caught his elbow.

"Dude, what is with you? Honestly, anyone would think you hate her the way you are always belittling her and barging in on our conversations."

Are you kidding me? Kyle sighed and shook his elbow free. But Lucas was right, he hadn't been very kind to her. The last thing he wanted to do was hurt her; he cared more for Harmony than Lucas gave him credit for, but no way was Kyle going to let him know that.

"Lucas, do yourself a favour and just let her go. I sincerely think that Harmony is either totally oblivious to your attempts to win her heart or completely uninterested. Maybe even both. Save your pride and don't get serious with her, okay?"

Lucas crossed his arms across his chest and eyed Kyle with mock defiance.

"Oh yeah? And you're telling me this as a friend or as an enemy?" Lucas shook his head and looked disgusted, although Kyle missed the glimmer of amusement in his eyes. "You know what the real issue here is? You are falling for your daughter's nanny, and you're all broken up because she likes me better that you."

Kyle could hardly believe his ears. Before he could recover from his shock, Lucas was already down the hall on his way out. "Coward," Kyle spat the word out violently before storming into his office.

Chapter Eleven

One afternoon, while Ellie was napping, Harmony found Marjorie reading a book in a little nook in the living room. She wasn't exactly sure if it would be considered impertinent to ask the question weighing on her heart, but she figured it couldn't do much harm.

"Marjorie," Harmony began, not quite sure how to voice her thoughts. "I just wanted to ask you, well, how is Kyle's relationship with God? I mean, he's okay with us taking Ellie to church every week and he's fine with us hosting the bible study here, but he seems to get uncomfortable whenever the subject of God comes up."

When Harmony stopped to breathe, she realized Marjorie had adopted an unreadable expression. *Please don't let me offend her.*

"Of course, it's really none of my business, so don't feel obligated to tell me," Harmony hastened to explain.

"Sit down a moment dear," Marjorie motioned to a chair on her right, still with the strange, unnervingly calm expression in her face. She put her book away and then sighed, looking Harmony straight in the eyes.

"Kyle and Lily were not raised in a Christian home. It was neither a happy nor comforting atmosphere. Their father divorced me shortly after I became a Christian, and I think that Kyle blamed me and my newfound faith for the divorce. Their father died in the military only a few years later, and it was extremely hard on both Kyle and Lily. Then Kyle went away to play minor league hockey."

Marjorie stopped for a moment and a glazed look came to her eyes, almost as if she had been transported to the past somewhere years ago. Harmony waited patiently, knowing that Marjorie would explain the rest in due time. "I had a good job, and while Kyle was away playing hockey, Lily was constantly out and about at fashion shows, spas, and parties. Once Kyle was drafted to the NHL, he adopted a similar lifestyle of parties and fun. That was when he met Hilary, Ellie's mother."

A dark look came into Marjorie's eyes, and her next words came out through clenched teeth. "Kyle was not walking with the Lord, and unfortunately, it ended in her getting pregnant. That was shortly after he found out I had breast cancer and would need surgery." If possible, an even darker look entered Marjorie's eyes and a frown was etched between her eyebrows. "That woman—" Marjorie stopped abruptly. She shook her head. "I'm sorry. It's not my story to tell, and I'm not at the liberty of sharing details. Let's just say that Ellie was not born under the best of circumstances." Marjorie sighed. "I know that God has a plan for all of us and for each of our lives, but Kyle just doesn't want to believe that. He doesn't want to acknowledge that he doesn't have to do it alone." The sadness in Marjorie's voice nearly broke Harmony's heart.

Harmony reached forward and grabbed Marjorie's soft hand in her own.

"Just keep praying," she encouraged. "God knows exactly what He's doing. You just have to persevere and just keep showing Kyle what God's love is all about."

Marjorie looked up at her and smiled, wiping her eyes. "I thank God for bringing you into our lives, dear. You really are a blessing." Then she added rather mischievously, "I wouldn't mind having you for a daughter in-law."

Harmony's jaw literally dropped, and she could feel her face growing warm with colour. Before she even had the chance to stutter a reply, Lily, her unofficial new best friend, burst through the doorway.

"Harmony!" Lily called as she bounced over, looking nearly as young and carefree as Ellie. Harmony exhaled in relief and gratefully turned away from Marjorie, and her impossible wish, to face Lily.

Lily grabbed her arm in excitement. "Harmony, guess what? I just started going to this dance class—ballroom dance, of course— and I've been having so much fun, so I was thinking that you could come with me. Then we'd be having so much fun together!" Lily giggled and Harmony felt overjoyed to see her friend looking so happy, happier than Harmony had seen her since she arrived at the Taylor House.

"Well, I've never really danced before, but I would like to try."

Lily actually squealed in delight. It reminded Harmony of the few movies she'd seen about teenage girls in high school, and she was amazed to find that that teenage girl lived in all women, even twenty-seven-year-old women. Lily grabbed her hand and dragged her towards the doorway.

"Quick, let's go tell Kyle, even though it doesn't concern him. He likes to be kept informed," Lily stated, rolling her eyes. Lily led Harmony to Kyle's office, but unfortunately, he was not there, so they went to the next most likely place: the kitchen. There they found Kyle and Ellie enjoying a midafternoon snack.

Harmony's heart lifted and she couldn't stop the smile that spread across her face when she saw the way Kyle was interacting with Ellie. He had two pieces of celery in his mouth and was barking like a walrus, keeping Ellie in fits of laughter.

"Kyle?" Lily gaped at him, obviously not accustomed to seeing her brother this way.

"Yeth?" Kyle turned to them, the celery sticks still hanging out of his mouth. It took all the self-control Harmony possessed not to burst out laughing at the look on his face. Kyle seemed to realize that he still had the celery sticks in his mouth, and he quickly swiped them out and tossed them onto his otherwise empty plate.

"Yes, Lily?" Kyle turned back to them, and if he felt any embarrassment over being caught imitating a walrus, he didn't show it.

Lily stared at him, clearly taken aback by his public display of fatherly affection. Harmony couldn't have been happier to see how comfortable Ellie had become around her dad.

"Uh...dancing, right." Lily blinked twice, coming out of her apparent stupor and proceeding to tell Kyle of their plans to go dancing.

"Dear wonderful, great, and awesome brother," she began sarcastically, completely recovered from her earlier shock, "may we poor slaves, who are but dogs, please leave the premises tonight to go to dance class?" Lily bowed at the waist before adding a cheeky "your grace." Always with a flair for the dramatic, Lily was quite comical, and she obviously knew how to annoy her brother.

Kyle glared at her and then turned to Harmony. "I thought we were going to watch a movie with Ellie tonight?" It came out more as an accusation than a question, making Harmony cringe.

"Well, I can stay if you want me to. I—" Harmony didn't get to finish because Lily cut her off.

"Oh no, brother dear! The poor girl has worked selflessly and tirelessly for so long. You must let poor Cinderella go to the ball. Surely, you would not be so cruel as to deny her this one simple pleasure. And besides," Lily switched from cajoling to accusatory in six seconds flat, "since when does she have to run her whole life by you? I mean, can't the girl even get a half-day off? Like seriously, how long has she been working here, going on two months now, right? And when was the last time she did something fun for herself?"

There was a moment of strained silence when Marjorie entered the kitchen, and having heard the last comment, she broke the silence with a suggestion. "Here's a thought: why don't you all go? I can take care of the little munchkin." Marjorie leaned over and tickled Ellie under her chin, causing some more music-like giggles to pour from her tiny body.

"Well, Lucas was going to come over and hang with me after the munchkin had gone to bed," Kyle said reluctantly, dipping his head towards the laughing toddler.

"Well, invite him too," Marjorie chirped. "The more, the merrier."

Kyle muttered something about hoping Lucas was busy, which surprised Harmony. She wasn't sure why inviting Lucas would bother him so much. But she had noticed the way Kyle's attitude towards Lucas had changed drastically in the past few weeks, and it was even worse if she was around. A slow smile spread across her lips. Was it possible that Kyle was jealous of the time she spent with Lucas?

Guilt and shame hit her like a slap in the face at the thought. What was she thinking? It didn't matter what Kyle thought of her; she wasn't free to even think about pursuing a relationship with him.

Roger's death still haunted her, Kyle didn't care about God, and she knew she wanted a husband who would build her up in the faith, not drag her down. She looked at Kyle with mixed feelings, hoping that he'd decide not to come with them and wishing that he'd say yes all at the same time.

"I…guess I could give him a call," Kyle said reluctantly.

Chapter Twelve

Harmony looked at herself in the mirror while holding a simple blue dress against her frame. Someone knocked on the door.

"Come in," Harmony called.

Lily opened the door, wrapped in a silk housecoat with her hair all piled up on her head and her makeup done so extravagantly Harmony would not have believed she did it herself, if she didn't know her as well as she did.

Lily looked at the dress in Harmony's hands and raised both her delicately shaped eyebrows. "That's what you were going to wear?" Laughter bubbled from her lips. "This class is black tie, sweetie. Don't you have anything a little...well, you know, black tie-ish?"

Harmony shook her head.

"I've never heard of dance class being black tie," she responded doubtfully.

"Okay, so it's not black tie, black tie, but still, you can't wear that," Lily made a face of mock horror. "What would the guys think?"

Harmony laughed, but she didn't have anything else to wear. She was a missionary's daughter, and her parents had never put much emphasis on material things, least of all clothing. She and Lily were polar opposites. It really was amazing that they were becoming such good friends. But just thinking about what Kyle would think made her want to wear something prettier. Fancier. And that was not good at all.

Lily was looking a little amused when she held out her hand. "Follow me."

Lily lead her into her bedroom and threw open her closet doors.

Harmony stood at the entrance to Lily's walk-in closet, confusion etched on her features. "Lily," she called into the cavern of Lily's closet, "what are you doing?"

Lily couldn't possibly think that anything in her closet would fit Harmony. Well, maybe on her arm. Whereas Lily was barely a size two, Harmony wasn't anywhere close to single digits. She smiled to herself, wondering what Lily was going to come up with.

"Okay, so I have this friend," Lily called from inside her closet, "and I thought you might like something a little fancier, so I called her and she lent me some dresses." Lily emerged, holding five black dresses. "I think she wears the same size as you, so I thought, why not do a makeover?"

Harmony laughed, grabbing one of the dresses. "Okay, but let's not get too crazy." Eventually, Harmony settled on one of the more conservative flowy dresses that Lily said would be perfect for dancing. She wore her own black pumps and Lily took care of her hair and makeup, promising that she wouldn't go overboard. Lily herself wore a spaghetti-strap dress that had a flowy knee-length skirt paired with some impressive diamond jewelry. Harmony put on her standard cross necklace and a simple gold coloured bracelet.

Harmony lifted a hand to her hair, looking at herself in the mirror. "Do I look all right?" she asked softly. Harmony couldn't help but wonder what Kyle would think of her dress. She knew she really shouldn't—couldn't—care, but she did. And she wasn't quite sure what to do about it.

Kyle looked in the mirror as he buttoned up his crisp-white dress shirt. He put on the silver cuff links his mom had bought him and picked out a simple grey tie. He didn't mind dressing up and he was used to it, since players had to wear suits for hockey games, but he chuckled when he thought of Lucas and how much he hated wearing dress clothes. Lucas was such a laid-back guy; he was completely out of his element when it came to fashion. Kyle could only imagine his sister's reaction if Lucas showed up in jeans. As long as Lucas didn't try to flirt with Harmony, Kyle didn't care one bit what he decided to wear.

Kyle slipped on his jacket and looked at himself one last time in the mirror. Not too shabby. He wondered what Harmony would think. As long as she thought he looked better than Lucas... *Knock it off, Taylor,* he cautioned himself. *Just being honest.* He grinned and was about to exit his room when his cell phone rang. For the fourth time. So, he might have been rejecting Cassandra's calls, but seriously, they had had a meeting less than a week ago. What could be so important that she needed to call him *four times*? Kyle decided he had better answer it just in case.

"Hello?"

"Oh, Kyle, you would not believe how long I've been trying to get a hold of you," Cassandra said breathlessly. Kyle rolled his eyes.

"What's so important, may I ask?" He really did try to keep the sarcasm out of his voice, but Cassandra always had a way of getting to him.

"Well, I was wondering if you had time for a quick meeting. I could pick you up and we could go to that new grill I was telling you about to go over some minor details of your new endorsement contract."

"Why would we do that when I have a perfectly good office here? And besides, whenever we go anywhere, we get no work done and all you want to talk about is Har—Ellie's nanny." There was dead silence on the other end of the phone. Well, that was a first. Then Cassandra's nervous laughter made its way to his ear.

"Oh, Kyle. You really are a scream."

Kyle rolled his eyes again and sighed. He glanced at his watch.

"Listen, Cassandra. We will have to get together another time. I have to go or I'm going to be late."

"Late for what?"

Kyle mentally kicked himself. Famous last words. "Dancing, I'm going to dance class," he mumbled. Hopefully that would ward off any future questions. Knowing Cassandra, probably not.

"Can I come?"

Great. Just what he needed. Because he so desperately wanted to go dancing with his agent. Who just happened to be driving him crazy.

"Um, sorry, Cassandra..." Kyle said, looking for a way out of the mess he'd gotten himself into. "My phone...dying... Can't hear..." Kyle said in an over exaggerated manner and then ended the call. Then he proceeded to turn off his phone. He might even decide to leave it at home. In hindsight it was pretty mean to just hang up on her like that but what could he say. He really didn't want to go dancing with Cassandra.

Kyle made his way down to the foyer where they were all meeting. He sat down on the bench by the huge double doors and waited for the girls to be ready. How long does it take for two girls to get dressed? Just then, the doorbell rang and in came Lucas. Kyle's eyes nearly bulged out of his head. Not only was Lucas *willingly* wearing a suit; he was wearing a tie, and not just any tie, but a bow tie. And his hair was slicked back. And...boy, was he wearing a lot of cologne. It was amazing that Kyle hadn't smelled him before he even made it to the door.

"Who are you and what have you done with my best friend?"

Lucas laughed, but he tugged his tie uncomfortably. "So," he asked as he looked around the room, "where are the ladies?"

Kyle was just about to answer when Lily strutted down the stairs.

"Wow, Lil. Don't you think that outfit is a bit much?"

He wanted to slap a hand over his mouth the instant he said the words, but he couldn't help it; they just popped out. Kyle couldn't believe that the beautiful woman standing there was his annoying, bratty little sister. She shot him a glare that could counter global warming and came over to greet Lucas. Kyle thought he was going to be sick when he saw how she was fluttering her eyelashes at Lucas. Lucas. Of all people, it had to be Lucas. And whoa...you could drown a rat in the amount of perfume she was wearing. Could this night get any weirder?

Just then, Kyle's attention was captured by the angel descending the spiral staircase. His breath caught in his throat, and he was certain that his heart nearly skipped a beat. Scratch that. His heart stopped beating altogether. Harmony was wearing a stunning black dress that shimmered in the light. She had shiny black heels on her feet, and the skirt of her flowy dress ended just below the knee. The dress had a cowl neckline and was completely figure-flattering in every sense of the word.

Kyle had to make a conscious effort to close his gaping mouth. Their gazes locked, and he went straight back into cardiac arrest. He could see Harmony's complexion change even under the blush his sister had no doubt insisted on her wearing.

When he came back to his senses, he heard Lucas going on and on about how beautiful she looked. Kyle gritted his teeth and breathed slowly. It wouldn't really make much sense for him to punch his best friend in the face for no good reason at all. Especially when he was complimenting someone. Kyle turned around and was just about to reach for the door handle when a soft little voice from the back of the room made him stop.

"Daddy, you can't go witout a goodbye kiss!" Ellie launched herself from the hall, where she had been standing, into his arms. All the anger, jealousy, and uncertainty melted away as he held his daughter in his arms. She was all that mattered, the most important part of him. Ellie leaned over and gave him a peck on the cheek.

"I wove you, Daddy," she whispered in his ear.

"I love you too, sweetheart." Kyle's voice was husky with emotion as he put her down and sent her off to find "Grammy."

"Wow, wasn't that nice? She forgot to say goodbye to the rest of us in the halo of your excellence." Lily's words were laced with sarcasm and even maybe a bit of jealousy. Kyle tried to bite back the cutting retort on the tip of his tongue, but he probably would not have succeeded had Harmony not stepped in.

"I thought that was really sweet. Anyway, hadn't we better go now?"

Lucas hurried to agree with her, and they all made their way down the walkway to Kyle's car. Kyle couldn't help feeling pleased when Harmony ended up sitting beside him in the front passenger seat. As they started on their way, Lucas broke the silence.

"So, Harmony, have you ever been dancing before?"

"We learned some Indonesian folk dances, but I've never done any ballroom dancing," Harmony replied.

"We?" Kyle probed. Out of the corner of his eye, he could see Harmony's face darken with sorrow.

"My parents and I," she said in a choked voice. "And... Roger." Harmony whispered the name, just barely loud enough for him to hear. Her fiancé, whose death she had yet to come to terms with. His heart ached to comfort her, to take away the pain. Kyle cleared his throat and tried to suppress his feelings.

"So, do you have any siblings?" Lucas asked.

"Yes, I have a twin sister, Melody." Harmony sounded relieved at the new subject and Kyle could understand why.

"Wait, what's her name?" Lily called from the back of the car.

"Oh, her name's Melody," Harmony repeated.

There was a moment of stunned silence, followed by an eruption of laughter that filled the vehicle.

"You're joking, right?" Lucas asked skeptically.

Harmony shook her head and pulled out her phone. She handed it back to Lily and Lucas. "This was taken a few years ago when I came back to Canada on furlough."

"Wow," Lily commented. "You two look nothing alike."

"But really, is her name actually Melody?" Lucas asked for the second time as he looked closely at the phone in his hand. "I mean, Harmony and Melody, isn't that a bit, well, you know..."

Harmony laughed and smiled at Lucas, though Kyle could see that it never reached her eyes. "You mean, weird? Well, my dad always said it was that or Ebony and Ivory."

Lucas, Lily, and Harmony laughed at that.

"I still haven't seen the picture yet," Kyle reminded them. He was really interested in seeing what Harmony's twin sister looked like. At the next red light, Harmony held out her phone. Kyle looked over to see Harmony with her arm slung around a woman who could not have been more different. Though similar in height and build, this woman had short and spiky black hair that had streaks of bright green throughout. Her face was loaded with makeup and her clothing looked expensive and slightly over-the-top. Her eyes were the exact same hue of Caribbean blue as Harmony's but lacked all the warmth and love that was so abundant in Harmony's. She was pretty, but she did not hold a candle to Harmony's natural, wholesome beauty.

"She's very pretty," Kyle said, not exactly sure what he was supposed to say yet knowing it should be something. "And you're right, you two look nothing alike." He thought Harmony was about to say something when Lily cried out, "There it is!"

Kyle wondered why he felt like he had just been saved by the bell. Was it the way Harmony's expression darkened only half a minute ago?

Chapter Thirteen

Harmony felt nervous as they walked into the large room with mirrors covering one wall and chairs lined up on the other. She was glad that she had Lily by her side; she couldn't imagine how out of place she would feel if she'd showed up by herself.

Lily chattered away happily, not even needing any response other than an "uh-huh" or "oh." Harmony usually appreciated her happy chatter, but tonight, something just kept nagging at the edge of her mind. Kyle had said her sister was pretty. Harmony felt so frustrated and confused. Why would something like that bother her? What a stupid thing to obsess about. Granted, she knew that Mel was gorgeous, and from all accounts—mainly from Melody herself—talented and totally chic. And why on earth did that matter to her? She closed her eyes and sighed. *Lord, please help me. I don't understand the feelings I am feeling and they are not in my nature. Help me not be ruled by emotions but by your Holy Spirit. Amen.*

Lily tapped her on the shoulder.

"You okay? You looked like you'd fallen asleep."

Harmony smiled and shook her head. "No, I'm not asleep yet."

Lily laughed and nodded towards a group of guys. "See anyone interesting?"

Harmony giggled and gave Lily a friendly shove. "I came to learn to dance, not pick up guys."

Lily gave her a look of mock horror. "Where's the fun in that?"

"So, how does this dancing thing work?" Harmony asked, effectively changing the subject.

Lily started to explain to her about how the dance class worked and how everyone was put into partners, but Harmony's attention was drawn elsewhere. She gaped as she watched Kyle and Lucas standing amidst a crowd of women who were apparently thrilled to meet two famous hockey players. Women were handing them napkins to sign, gushing about how tall or handsome they were and, quite frankly, throwing themselves at two somewhat bemused hockey players. Harmony turned wide-eyed to Lily.

"Lily, look at this. Do women do that all the time?"

Lily looked up and shrugged. "Yeah, but don't worry. The guys are used to it. It happens whenever they go out."

Harmony was shocked. To think that grown women would just throw themselves at men like Lucas and Kyle, not because they were nice guys or they were funny with a good sense of humor, but because they were rich, famous hockey players.

"Well, that's just wrong," Harmony exclaimed fervently. Lily stepped back with a laugh.

"Whoa, girl. Who would have thought you'd have such a hot temper?"

Harmony could feel the heat rushing to her face. "I don't have a temper," she protested weakly. Lily eyed her mockingly and cradled her chin with her hand as though deep in thought. She circled around Harmony like a lioness circling her prey.

"But what might have brought this on, I wonder?" Lily stopped and appeared to be thinking about it when a light bulb seemed to light up over her head and she smiled mischievously, even while emotion darkened her chocolate-brown eyes.

"So, you like Lucas, huh?"

Harmony felt the tension ooze out of her. "I don't like Lucas. At least not like that."

"Aha!"

Harmony jumped back, surprised at her friend's sudden outburst. "You like Kyle, you like Kyle, you like Kyle," Lily chanted in a singsong voice. Harmony could feel herself blush.

"Lily, be quiet. I don't. I don't like Kyle."

Lily grinned and waggled her eyebrows. "Ah, but you do, my fair maiden. You do." Lily sighed and clutched her heart dramatically while pretending to swoon. "How terribly romantic."

Harmony had never wished to strangle anyone before—okay, so she rarely wanted to strangle anyone, but she was getting mighty close to it.

"Now I see why Kyle finds you annoying," Harmony snapped then immediately became ashamed of herself. Lily looked at her blankly for a second then smiled.

"See?" she said dreamily. "You'd be a perfect couple!"

"Oh, stop it," Harmony replied, exasperated but laughing at Lily's antics in spite herself. "I never said I liked Kyle."

"Well, why else would you be so protective over the guys?" Lily challenged.

"Because...because..." Harmony racked her brains, searching for a plausible reason. "Because they are my friends. They're basically like brothers to me."

Harmony almost winced at that barely veiled lie. The feelings she had for Kyle were far from sisterly. *Yeah, that was a stretch, even for someone in denial,* Harmony's split personality seemed to say. *I am not in denial!* Harmony argued with herself. *Are to. Am not. Are to. Am not. Listen, honey, deNile ain't just a river. Oh, you are impossible.* Harmony placed a hand to her forehead. Okay, having conversations with herself was definitely not a good sign. This job seemed to be threatening her sanity.

"Ha! Brother my foot. You like him. Admit it."

"Never," Harmony shot back laughingly, hoping to bring the conversation back to a less personal subject. Suddenly, Lily's eyes widened and her jaw dropped as she focused on something behind Harmony.

"Incoming!" Lily turned away abruptly, and before Harmony even had a chance to wonder what was going on, she felt a tap on her shoulder.

"Good evening, madam."

Harmony turned to face a tall, skinny man with dark greasy hair and small beady black eyes. She was ashamed to admit that her first response to the man was negative. She imagined he was a nice enough man. Probably. He looked to be at least a couple decades older than she was, and she didn't like the way he invaded her personal space. The look he gave her made her skin crawl.

Harmony managed a small smile of greeting, looking around desperately for Lily. A little bit of warning would have been nice.

"I don't believe I've seen you here before. I'm sure I would have remembered meeting such a vision." The man bowed over her hand and placed a kiss on the back of it before she pulled it away, wrapping her arms around herself and taking a step away from him. "Marvin Collins at your service."

"Thank you. It's nice to meet you too. I'm sorry. I really need to get back to my friends—"

"You're not even going to tell me your name?" Marvin asked her, taking a step towards her.

Harmony took another step back, trying her best to think of a way to make him leave her alone without being rude. Her sister would have told him to get lost the moment he had the gall to introduce himself, but Harmony tended to be more sensitive to other people's feelings. Lot of good that did her.

"My name's Harmony, but my friends are probably looking for me and I should—"

"Would you do me the honour of allowing me to be your dance partner for the evening?"

Harmony's mouth dropped open. "Um…"

She glanced around the room, looking for Kyle, Lily, Lucas, or anyone, but of course, none of them were in sight. Typical. She was still a little miffed at Lily for leaving her; didn't the woman know that there was safety in numbers? "That's really very sweet of you, but…" Harmony was wracking her brain for any excuse that she could come up with when Kyle appeared at her side, placing his hand protectively on the small of her back.

"Hey, hon," Kyle said, leaning over to give her a quick kiss on the cheek, nearly sending her heart into overdrive. "Are you ready?"

Kyle turned to Marvin, acting as if he'd only just noticed him standing there. "Oh, sorry. I don't know what I did with my manners." Kyle extended his hand and gave Marvin a winning smile. "I'm Kyle Taylor."

Blanching slightly, Marvin gingerly took Kyle's hand. "Marvin Collins. You...you're Kyle Taylor...the hockey player?"

"That's me," Kyle acknowledged, shooting Harmony a smile that made her forget everything and everyone else. Harmony stood mutely by his side, trying to sort out her errant thoughts. Kyle didn't mean anything by his kiss, his hand on her back, and his killer smile, even if they did wreak havoc on her insides. He was simply being his typical amazing self. *Breathe, Harmony. Breathe.*

Making a concentrated effort not to focus on Kyle's strong hand across her back, Harmony finally found her voice. "Oh, Kyle, I was just telling Marvin that since I already have you as my dance partner, I can't accept his gracious offer to be my partner for the evening." She looked up at Kyle, almost losing herself in his melted-chocolate eyes.

"Yes, we're already partners for the night," Kyle affirmed, pulling her closer to his side. Her legs turned to jelly, and it was amazing the she managed to remain standing. "Actually, we came with some friends, and we really should be getting back to them." With a nod in Marvin's direction, Kyle led Harmony across the dance floor to where Lily and Lucas stood waiting.

"Thanks for coming to my rescue back there," Harmony said shyly, pushing a lock of hair behind her ear. Kyle shrugged, sending her a grin that sent tingles all the way down to her toes.

"Not a problem, but I do expect you to be my dance partner for at least part of the night," he leaned closer to her and winked. "Wouldn't want to make a liar out of you."

Harmony started to smile back at him, when she realized just what she'd gotten herself into. This was her boss, her non-Christian boss whom she was way too attracted to. And she'd just agreed to be his dance partner? Talk about glutton for punishment.

As she and Kyle passed by Lily and Lucas, Lily mouthed, "You're welcome," and gave Harmony a wink.

Harmony sighed. *Well, here goes nothing.*

Kyle couldn't help but feel happy that *he* was the one who got to dance with Harmony, especially since he knew that Lucas had planned on asking her himself. Not that he was jealous or something, but you know, he had to protect her. Not that Lucas was a bad guy or anything, but him and Harmony…nah, they would never work.

Out of the blue, reality hit Kyle like a meteorite caught in the gravitational pull of a planet. What on earth was he doing here? This was his employee—his daughter's nanny for goodness' sakes. What exactly had possessed him to go over and kiss Harmony just to get her away from that Marvin guy?

Kyle groaned inwardly. *What have you gotten yourself into, Taylor?*

Kyle gazed down at Harmony. Her blue eyes looked dark like the night sky in the dim lighting of the dance studio, and stars seemed to sparkle in the watery depths of them. Okay, where did *that* thought come from? When did he become such a poet? Kyle could feel his hands become clammy. Man, did this place have no air-conditioning?

Come on, Taylor, he ordered himself. *You're just dancing. What's the big deal? It's not like you're new at this or something.* Kyle tried to think of something to say to Harmony to make a conversation but he couldn't think of anything. Not one single thing. Aside from that, he felt as though his mouth was full of sand. Seriously, what was wrong with him? Kyle cleared his throat, determined to overcome this illogical display of nervousness.

"So, Harmony, are you excited for your first dance class?"

Harmony looked up at him and gave him a slight smile. It nearly sent his heart into overdrive. *Must be that salsa I had with supper. Yeah, that's it,* Kyle thought to himself.

"I hope it will be fun," she began, "but I have to warn you. I was born a klutz, and I don't think I will be any more graceful while dancing."

Kyle smiled and said, "Don't worry. I'll cover for you."

The woman in charge made a point to come over to Kyle and Harmony and Lucas and Lily to show them a few steps, seeing as they were drop ins. The steps she demonstrated would be a piece of cake for Kyle, but he wasn't so sure about Harmony. She looked flustered and refused to make eye contact with him. Kyle smiled slightly. She was cute when she was flustered. Granted, he really couldn't blame her; he was, after all, her boss. Yep, this was going to be a very interesting night.

Out of the corner of his eye, Kyle could see Lucas and Lily dancing. Or at least, trying to. Lily was laughing and giggling whenever they made a mistake and Lucas was obviously preoccupied. Doing what? Ogling Harmony and probably wishing that she was dancing with him. He wasn't even trying to be subtle about it.

The dance instructor then showed them a few more steps, talked about the proper way to have one's arms, how to spin, et cetera. Then she told them to try it with their partners. Kyle could feel the heat creeping up his neck. He had danced and partied a lot, especially when he first came to the NHL. Granted it hadn't been ballroom dancing, but still. And yet somehow this was different. Dancing with Harmony was somehow special and more meaningful than when he'd danced with other women. He wasn't sure why it mattered, but he didn't want to mess this up.

Come on, Taylor, he reminded himself. *It's only dancing.*
Right?

Harmony forced herself to focus on what the woman in charge was saying to her instead of Kyle's strong shoulder, on which her hand would soon be resting. He was extremely distracting with his gorgeous brown eyes and dazzling smile. Beside the fact that he was a very attractive man, he was kind. Caring. Compassionate. He was a great father and all in all, a really great guy. Unfortunately for her, that was the problem. No matter how good-looking someone was on the outside, in Harmony's perspective, that was all either enhanced or diminished by the person's character. Yet the better she got to know Kyle, the more appealing he became. But if they weren't united by faith in Christ, she couldn't even think about a future with Kyle.

Wait, a future with Kyle? She didn't have those types of feelings for Kyle, no, so what if he was handsome and funny and smart? She wasn't interested.

As she watched the lady in charge demonstrate the dance, she became more and more nervous. Just the thought of being held in Kyle's arms sent shivers to her spine. Nope, she wasn't interested at all. Well, she blamed Lily for this. If Lily hadn't left her at the mercy of Marvin and then oh-so-innocently sent Kyle to come rescue her, she wouldn't even be in this mess. Kyle's voice broke through her thoughts.

"Harmony? Are you ready?"

Harmony looked up at him and nodded. She could do this. It was one dance, just lessons. She could do this. *I can do all things through Him who strengthens me.* Harmony smiled to herself. Philippians chapter four verse thirteen. One of her favourites. She often marveled at how God had a way of bringing different verses to her mind when she needed them most.

She took a deep breath and got into her "stance." Harmony placed her left hand on Kyle's shoulder as he gently placed his right hand on the small of her back. The warmth of his touch sent tingles up and down her spine and she had to remind herself to keep her arms firm as opposed to melting against his chest. Music floated into the room from large speakers in each corner of the ceiling. Harmony was surprised at how well Kyle danced. Even she didn't trip or step on his toes. He was steady and he could lead.

"You're really good at this. Dancing, that is." Harmony tried to ease the tension by starting a conversation.

Kyle grinned, his gorgeous eyes twinkling, and said, "Thanks. I've had some practice."

Harmony was just about to respond when Lucas arrived and tapped Kyle on the shoulder.

"Mind if I cut in?" Lucas asked with a grin and a wink at Harmony.

For a minute, Kyle looked like he was about to tell Lucas that yes, he did mind. And for just a fraction of a moment, Harmony desperately hoped that he would. Instead, Kyle dropped his arms and stepped away from her, and although he frowned at Lucas, he only shrugged.

"Be my guest."

Harmony tried to ignore the hollow feeling that settled in the pit of her stomach as she watched him walk away. She had no reason and no right to harbour any feelings for Kyle. No matter how much she might like to.

"Whoa," Lucas's voice broke through her thoughts, as he pulled her into a slow waltz. "Did you see how angry he looked?"

Harmony glanced up in surprise. Lucas sounded happy about Kyle being angry. In fact, he looked pretty pleased with himself. She frowned slightly, puzzled.

"You do that on purpose don't you? You try to make him mad," Harmony accused. "Why?"

Lucas grinned at her. "You're good for him, you know that, Harmony?"

Harmony missed a step, taken aback at the strange turn the conversation seemed to have taken.

"I'm good for him? What does that have to do with—"

Harmony stopped abruptly when Lucas' meaning dawned on her. "No, Lucas. Kyle and I aren't...what I mean to say is..." Harmony sighed, stumbling over her words. "I'm Ellie's nanny, nothing more." And that was the way it had to stay.

Lucas shrugged, but he didn't look like he believed her in the least. "Whatever you say."

Focusing on something over her shoulder, Lucas blew out an exasperated breath. "Here comes trouble," he muttered quietly.

From the far corner of the room, Harmony heard a loud, high, rather affected voice saying, "Oh, Kyle. Who would have thought I'd run into you here!" Harmony glanced over her shoulder to see Cassandra—Kyle's agent right?—giggling at nothing at all with her arm entwined with a stunned and not too pleased-looking Kyle.

This was going to be a long night.

Chapter Fourteen

Kyle could not believe that Cassandra had actually followed him to dance class. How did she even find him? Surely, there were many different dance classes all over the city. And now she expected him to be pleased to see her? Come on.

Cassandra was looking up at him, her green eyes watery—crocodile tears, no doubt—and her chin wobbling.

"Kyle? Is everything all right? I... I thought you would be happy to see me. Your phone died at the most inopportune moment, but I was sure that you said it would be fine for me to come. I was a little late getting here, but..." She dipped her chin and let a single tear slide down her cheek. In a near whisper, she said, "I didn't realize you were avoiding me."

Wow, way to lay on the guilt trip. Now Kyle felt like the biggest jerk in history and he didn't like it. So he had pretended his phone died so as not to have to invite Cassandra dancing, but really, the woman could be very trying. Make that extremely trying. Like right now. Besides, he was almost positive that she was faking it. Almost.

"Avoiding you? What would give you that idea?" Kyle just barely masked the sarcasm in his voice. Cassandra looked up at him again, her chin jutted out defiantly and her eyes flaming with a rage that he'd never come across, at least not directed at him.

"You said you couldn't come to *work* with me and then you go out to party with your daughter's nanny. Very professional of you, Kyle," she said sneeringly.

Kyle rose to his full six foot three inches and looked down disdainfully at Cassandra. No way was he going to put up with that nonsense from her. What he did and didn't do was his business, and who was she to tell him he could not do something with someone because they worked for him? Didn't she, in a way, work for him?

"Listen very carefully to what I have to say, Cassandra. What I do with my time is my business, and if you have a problem with that, I can always find another agent."

Cassandra's eyes widened and she backed down, but she looked like she was about to recover when Kyle turned around and walked away. He was not going to wait around for her to come to her senses. He considered going over and cutting in on Harmony and Lucas but decided against it. Later, he might, but he figured it would be better to remove the spotlight from his "daughter's nanny." He didn't understand what Cassandra's problem was. So Harmony had come dancing with them, big whoop. It wasn't as though he was interested in her in a romantic way or anything.

Right? Yeah right. He didn't need another relationship, seeing that he was a single dad and was, well, awful at maintaining a healthy love relationship. Kyle sighed, trying to forget the past. Sometimes, ancient history was just not ancient enough.

That night, when they finally got back into the car and started on their way home, Kyle couldn't help but feel relieved. And frustrated. Along with more than a little bit angry. Never again was he going back to that dance studio. Judging by the silence that joined them in the vehicle on the way home, that same thought was going through everybody else's head too. The last hour after the actual lesson consisted of him cutting in on Harmony and Lucas, Cassandra cutting in on him and Harmony, Lily cutting in on Harmony and Lucas, and Lucas cutting in on him and Harmony in no consistent order. And the only one who seemed to be having a good time was, annoyingly, Lucas.

All in all, it was a very awkward, frustrating night out. Well, there was a first time for everything. Along with an inevitable last.

Chapter Fifteen

Four days after the disastrous dance night, Harmony received a phone call from her mother. This was the first call she had received from either of her parents since she had accepted the job as Ellie's nanny and returned to Canada. It did not surprise or bother her, because she knew that her parents served in a remote place with limited telephones or cell service.

"Hi, Mom," Harmony greeted Carol, her mother, over the phone. Carol exchanged a quick greeting before updating her on the rest of the work at the mission.

"And guess what, sweetheart, we are going on leave in a month or two. We are not exactly sure when, but we will be going throughout the country, explaining to churches the work we are doing down here. Yours is on the list!" Her mother cried happily. "I am so excited to be able to see you again. Your father and I have missed you." After a brief pause, Carol added, "And your sister too."

Harmony sighed and sank down onto the window seat in her room. The relationship between her sister and her parents had been strained ever since Melody decided to come back to Canada to finish high school and go to university instead of staying in Indonesia and joining the mission. That was part of the reason why Harmony decided against her sister's course and stayed with her parents. She knew how much working as a family overseas meant to them. Sometimes, she even wondered whether she'd been following God's path for her life or her parents'.

"Wow, Mom, That's great. I can't wait to see you again. And it would be great for you to meet Ellie. She's the sweetest little thing. I'm so glad I followed your advice and took the job here. It's been great." Accepting the job as a nanny for Ellie Taylor really had been one of the best choices she had made. Harmony couldn't remember the last time she'd felt so happy.

"That's wonderful honey. I am so glad." Her mother's voice then took on a sly tone as she asked, "What do you think about Kyle? I heard he is quite the heartthrob. Is he as handsome as the media portrays?" Harmony nearly dropped the phone; she was so surprised by her mother's question. Had her mother known Kyle was some rich and famous hockey player when she'd encouraged her to take this job? Why hadn't she told Harmony? Had her mom been setting her up? Whatever the case may be, she didn't want to be discussing Kyle with her mother, especially when she still wasn't sure of her own feelings towards him.

"Mom," Harmony began, ready to ask Carol exactly what she knew about Kyle when she heard Carol chuckle over the phone.

"All right, all right. Don't tell me. I'm sure I'll find out soon enough."

Carol then asked about Ellie and other less personal—no, less intimidating?—subjects. Carol's question about Kyle stirred up Harmony's confusing—and unwanted—feelings. Yes, Kyle was good-looking as well as funny, kind, caring, and strong. She smiled when she thought of how he'd rescued her from Marvin at dance class. He was her knight in shining armour, everything she'd never known she'd wanted.

Harmony mentally shook herself and tried to focus on what her mother was telling her, but thoughts of Kyle crowded her mind. She would never marry a man who didn't share her faith, but she was surprised at the depth of her feelings for Kyle. Harmony pressed a trembling hand to her forehead, barely even registering her mother's voice over the phone.

Oh, God. I think I'm falling in love with him. What am I going to do? To make matters worse, though it still hurt to think of Roger, she could no longer clearly imagine his face. When she closed her eyes, all she saw was Kyle, with his warm brown eyes smiling down at her.

Lord, help me.

Forty-five minutes later, she was off the phone and deep in prayer.

*****

Kyle was in the changeroom after practice with the rest of the guys when someone asked an odd question.

"So, Kyle, I hear you have new nanny. She nice, this nanny?" The question caught Kyle off guard since he didn't even remember telling anyone about Harmony. The only guys who had met her had been the seven or eight guys who had come to his house for the football game. Boris Domashevich, an immigrant from Russia who was still learning English, seemed to see the question on his face, for he added, "Lucas said so."

"He also said you're a bit controlling of this new employee. Any good reason?" Another guy from the back of the room piped up.

Lucas had been going around talking about stuff like that behind his back? Kyle couldn't help feeling betrayed. And he was not controlling. Okay, well, he got a little fired up when Lucas was being a flirt or a suck-up, but hey, that didn't mean he was controlling, did it?

"I am not controlling. She is in charge of taking care of my daughter. We already discussed time off, and if she wants any extra time, all she has to do is clear it with me, okay?" Kyle sounded harsher than he meant to, but the fact that Lucas was going around talking to the other guys about how he interacted with Harmony had him all riled up. There was silence in the locker room while Boris seemed to be considering what he said.

"Fair enough. You boss, she employee. Makes sense."

"Still, rumor has it you—oh I don't know—are maybe romantically interested in this new, pretty nanny."

That comment was the beginning of the downward spiral. Suddenly, everyone wanted to know if he liked the new nanny and whether or not she was cute.

"Okay, let's get this straight once and for all. I have no other interest in Harmony except that she is my daughter's nanny. Got it?"

Nothing he said made any difference. All the guys just wanted to give him a ribbing about liking his daughter's nanny, whether it was true or not. Kyle knew it was all in good-natured fun, but his feelings for Harmony were…complicated. He really couldn't decide how he felt about her, and having his whole team tease him definitely was not helping his case. Kyle might have snapped had it not been for good old Scott Little.

"Come on, guys. Leave him alone. She's his employee. No need to read anything more into this than is necessary."

Kyle was thankful for Scott standing up for him, but he was still having trouble keeping his cool. He got up in a huff, slung his bag over his shoulder, and he made his way to the parking lot which was reserved for the players. Kyle had always thought that girls were the ones who gossiped and backstabbed.

By the time Kyle got home, his anger had cooled considerably, and when he considered it, him and Harmony as a couple was not such a bad idea. Whoa, what was he thinking? Was he nuts? *Took a few too many hits to the head, Taylor,* he thought to himself. But the thought persisted and grew, and eventually, he could even picture a life with Harmony at his side. With them all, being a real family. Forever. *Okay, that's enough. Knock it off right now.*

Kyle parked his car and walked in through the main doors, closing the door quietly behind him. Kyle shook his head in an effort to clear it when lo and behold, the woman in question came over to greet him. She was wearing simple black jeans and a long-sleeved sweater the same blue as her eyes. Kyle's breath caught in his throat. Her blond hair was streaked with gold that shone in the dim light of the darkened hallway, matching the pure, kind heart of gold within her. Oh boy, was he in trouble.

"Kyle." Her soft voice seemed to float towards him on a cloud of loveliness. A cloud of loveliness? Yep, it was official. He had completely lost his mind.

"You are just in time. I let Ellie stay up a little later than usual because she wanted you to tuck her in tonight."

Kyle glanced at his watch. Sure enough, it was fifteen minutes past Ellie's bedtime. "Kyle? That's fine with you, right?"

Kyle looked up at her and nodded. No way could he let himself get caught up in her dazzling blue eyes. Or her breathtaking smile. Or her inner beauty that shone like the sun.

"Yeah, sure. Thanks for letting me know." Kyle forced his mind to focus on his daughter and not Harmony. He turned and bounded up the stairs two at a time. Only when he reached the top platform did he allow himself to look back at Harmony just one last time before he headed in to say goodnight to his daughter.

As he ducked through the doorway of Ellie's bedroom, he was awed at how their father-daughter relationship had changed. Just a few months ago, Ellie would have wanted anyone but him to come tuck her in…and he had been oblivious, not even knowing what he was missing by not spending time with his daughter and letting her know how much he loved her. Ellie sat up in bed when she noticed him come in and reached out for a hug. Kyle complied and kissed her forehead, smoothing back her sleek, curly blond hair with his hand.

"Good night, sweetheart," Kyle said, ready to put her to bed.

"But Daddy," Ellie whined, "I need to say my pwayers."

Kyle had forgotten that Harmony always prayed with Ellie.

"Okay," Kyle said, thinking fast. "You say your prayers and I'll listen."

Ellie nodded her head before folding her hands prayerfully and tucking them under her chin.

Kyle only half-listened until she mentioned something that shook him to the core. "And I pway dat you will make Miss Hawmony my mommy and…" Kyle could not believe his ears. When Ellie finished her prayers, Kyle broached the subject.

"Sweetheart," he began, not exactly sure how to explain this to Ellie without hurting her. "Miss Harmony can't be your Mommy."

Ellie frowned and shook her head in question. She looked up at him with her big brown innocent eyes and asked the question of the hour: "Why not?"

Such a simple question and yet… Kyle could not think of a single reason why not.

"Because…because that would mean that me and Miss Harmony would have to get married," Kyle explained, hoping that would stem the flow of any further questions from his three-year-old daughter. Ellie raised her eyebrows in question, like she had no doubt seen Harmony do many times before, and gave him a little smile.

"What's wong wit dat?"

Not a single thing.

"Well, um, it just isn't going to happen."

Ellie's frown deepened and she looked frustrated, even a bit exasperated. Any other day, it would have taken everything in him not to burst out laughing at her expression, but somehow, this conversation didn't make him feel like laughing.

"But I wove her and she woves me, and she woves you too and you wove her, wight?" She looked up at him inquisitively and then smiled and patted his cheek. "Dat's okay, Daddy. You didn't know, but God always answers our pwayers."

Kyle felt a pang in his chest when he thought of the pain that expectation would bring to his daughter. He could think of many unanswered prayers that he had uttered in the past, and had they been answered he would have been saved from many disappointments. *God, please don't let Mom and Dad get a divorce. God, please don't let my dad die. God, don't let it be true that Mom has breast cancer.* All unanswered prayers. How could anyone put their trust in a God who either didn't listen or didn't care? In the back of his mind, Kyle thought of the only prayer that was answered, one he hadn't even let himself say out loud, but proceeded to change his life in the best possible way: *God, please don't let her kill my baby.* With that final thought, Kyle bit back the bitter response on the tip of his tongue that was sure to crush whatever faith his daughter might have and just smiled.

"Sure thing, baby," he answered. "You've got to go to sleep now. Good night. I love you."

Ellie burrowed under the covers and smiled up at him. "I wove you de mostest."

Kyle left her bedroom with his heart feeling heavy and light at the same time. Funny thing was, all these conflicting emotions and self-evaluation started the moment Harmony came through his office doors.

Chapter Sixteen

There was a crisis in the Taylor household. Mookie was missing. It wasn't exactly a rare occurrence, but now he'd been missing in action for nearly sixteen hours. Harmony remembered on one occasion she'd found the ferret in her sock drawer. Marjorie had told her that as long as a door was open just a crack, Mookie would no doubt go in to explore. Her door had stayed closed ever since.

Mookie had gone missing the night before, and this morning when he had not been found, Ellie had been almost hysterical, crying and refusing to be comforted until Harmony made the little girl a cup of her now famous hot chocolate. Even then, after a couple of hours of searching to no avail, Harmony had to promise to search for him high and low while the little girl took her nap before Ellie began to calm down. To Harmony, it was worth it to see her little princess happy again.

Good as her word, Harmony set out to find Mookie only moments after Ellie was safely sleeping in her room. Harmony periodically checked her watch, estimating how much time she would have before Ellie woke up from her nap. Harmony thought she saw a flash of brown around the corner ahead of her when she ran head on into a very unhappy fake blond. What was Cassandra doing here? Why was she constantly hanging around the house?

"Watch where you're going," Cassandra snapped angrily.

Harmony chose to ignore the woman's rude behavior. After all, she was going to bible study that evening and needed to be loving and kind to everyone for the sake of Christ. Harmony groaned inwardly. You'd think that after growing up as a missionary she'd have that down pat. Wrong.

"Oh, Cassandra," Harmony greeted her, trying desperately to keep the edge out of her voice. "I didn't see you there. I was wondering, have you seen Mookie by any chance? He's missing and I really need to get him back."

Cassandra looked at Harmony as if she smelled something vile. "You think I would even notice if such a creature passed me? I have no time for that stupid animal." And in a huff, the resentful woman stormed off, leaving Harmony in the metaphoric dust.

Harmony had almost laughed out loud when Cassandra claimed that she wouldn't even notice Mookie. On one of her visits—which also happened for no apparent reason—she stood on a chair and screamed when Mookie ran into the room unaccompanied by his master.

Harmony always tried to be friendly, but it was useless. The woman hated her. She wasn't quite sure what she had ever done to Cassandra, except maybe wake up every morning. The only logical thing to do would be to avoid the woman whenever possible. Unfortunately, knowing Cassandra, that would be nearly impossible.

Oh, how Cassandra hated the beautiful, innocent, attractive blonde. She always had to act so sweet and so kind, just trying to suck up to Kyle. It made Cassandra sick just to watch. Well, she would not try to win brownie points with the boss, no. She preferred to be more direct. She was on her way to find Kyle, who was, of course, the reason of her visit.

Cassandra sauntered over to Kyle's office when she heard something that nearly stopped her heart. The tap, tap, tap of tiny little feet, not child-size but smaller, much smaller. Ferret-size. Cassandra took a few slow breaths to calm her racing heart and peeked around the corner. There it was, the long snake-like vermin scurrying around while looking for any small dark hidey hole to curl up in. Disgusting.

Out of the corner of her eye, Cassandra noticed a small empty wastebasket, and in a fit of courage, she snapped it up and slammed it down over the creature, imprisoning it in the dome-shaped object. As Cassandra looked down on the small metal garbage can, her pride and bravado melted away and were quickly replaced by anger. Anger directed towards the blond-haired, blue-eyed beauty pretending to look after the child and her things. That included her pet ferret. Well, she would see that that Harmony got exactly what she deserved. Would she tell Kyle? No. If he didn't get mad, that wouldn't make her look like she was a concerned friend, but a selfish, conniving, cruel, tattletaling woman. That was sure to impress him.

Cassandra looked around as if searching for an answer to her question in the hallway. Surprisingly, she actually found it. Just in front of her was a door, and that door led to Kyle's office. Kyle would hate it if anything happened to his office.

"Well, isn't it a pity that Harmony hasn't found you yet?" Cassandra said maliciously to the rodent trapped under the garbage can. "She won't be able to stop you from doing this."

Just as Cassandra was about to slide the garbage can over to Kyle's office, Marjorie appeared in the hallway. Cassandra wasn't exactly certain, but she always got the feeling that Marjorie didn't like her. Not a good start if she was going to be Cassandra's future mother-in-law. Once Kyle finally proposed that is.

"Cassandra, back again so soon? Why, we never even have time to miss you."

Cassandra managed a small smile. Thankfully, Marjorie did not stay to chat but just continued on her way, only stopping to check the time in the huge grandfather clock situated at the end of the hallway.

Cassandra breathed a sigh of relief. She turned back towards the metal trash can and slid it through the door of Kyle's office with her foot, not wanting to risk the thing getting free and touching her. Once safely behind closed doors, Cassandra set to work. She looked through Kyle's desk drawers and chose fifteen or so pages that she knew she had copies of, so that once the storm had passed she could kindly offer to print him out a new set. She set those papers aside for the moment and put the other papers out of order, threw them out of the drawers, letting them come to rest on the floor under Kyle's desk. Once she was happy with the hectic, disorganised array of papers, she turned back to the fifteen she had set aside and ripped them to shreds.

She looked back and surveyed her work, imagining Kyle's face when he saw this. She didn't want to be in Harmony's shoes when that time came. All the same, she wished she could stay to watch the fireworks. Cassandra carefully crept over to the metal basket in which the little rat was imprisoned and kicked it over with her foot. The ferret scurried out from underneath and went exactly where she would have put him herself, crawling under the desk.

Job well done, Cassandra. Job well done, she said to herself, wishing she could see what happened to poor little Harmony when Kyle found this mess. Cassandra hoped that she would be fired on the spot.

Once she made sure that there was no one in the hallway, she made her escape, shutting the door behind her. Wouldn't want that lovely little ferret to escape. And with that final thought, she exited from the foyer, got in her car, and drove away.

Harmony had looked everywhere. She'd look in all the common rooms, washrooms, bedrooms, and more. She'd checked every cupboard, drawer, and closet in the house, and still, she found nothing. Every room with an open door or even if the door was only slightly ajar, she'd looked in. She'd even searched every nook and cranny in the hall cleaning closet. And still, she had found nada, zip, nothing.

There was really only one place left to look: Kyle's office. She wasn't supposed to go in there, but she felt that this was an emergency. Harmony was pretty sure that Kyle would be in there anyway, so she would just go in and ask him if he had seen Mookie and if he minded her checking around in his office. He always seemed to disappear there. How much paperwork could a hockey player have? She knocked on the door but was surprised to hear no reply. After a moment's hesitation, she opened the door and entered.

"Kyle?"

Harmony gasped when she saw the room. It was completely trashed. There was paper strewn everywhere, on the floor, on the desk. There were even bits and pieces of paper ripped to shreds on the floor and around the desk. Harmony was shocked. She could not even imagine Mookie wreaking such havoc. Why, he could barely drag more than one paper at one time, and only when he really wanted to. Besides, these papers were ripped, not gnawed.

Her suspicions rose and she paused on the threshold of the office, trying to decide whether or not to go find Kyle right away or wait and try to find Mookie first. After a moment of thought, she decided she'd check for Mookie first, and then afterwards, she'd go find Kyle and show him what had happened.

Harmony waded through the mess of papers on the floor and walked over to the desk at the back of the room, really the only reasonable place for a ferret to hide. She dropped down to her knees and crawled under the desk, pushing out each drawer and feeling behind it for a thin, furry body. Once she reached the lowest drawer on the right side, she felt it. The silly thing kept slipping out of her grasp. Harmony heard the sound of footsteps, joined by voices outside the door. How on earth was she supposed to explain this? She reached out her hand in behind the drawer, her fingers groping for the fury, snake-like creature. She almost…had him…

"What do you think you're doing?"

At the sound of Kyle's angry voice, she jumped, banging her head against the underside of his desk. She jerked her hand back, scraping her forearm against a sharp edge on the back of the drawer.

"Ow!"

Harmony held the back of her head with her left hand, cradling her right arm against her chest. She crawled out from under the desk, blinking up at Lucas and Kyle. Lucas looked concerned and was holding Mookie, whereas Kyle looked more than a little angry. Harmony could almost hear Ricky Ricardo saying the famous line from *I Love Lucy* reruns: "Lucy, you got some splaining to do!"

"What on earth are you doing in my office?" Kyle repeated his question, then added another one. "And what happened in here?"

Harmony was grasping at straws for a reasonable explanation, which was extremely difficult with Kyle's brown eyes, almost black with rage, boring into her. Lucas shot Kyle a dirty look.

"Dude, chill. I mean, who knew you could be so careless?"

Oh great. Wrong answer. Harmony nearly flinched as the words left Lucas's mouth. Kyle's expression darkened and he let out a growl-like sound and turned around. He turned back and pointed an accusing finger first at Lucas.

"Fine," he ground out the words, as if they came from clenched teeth. "You, fix this," Kyle said to Lucas before turning to her. "And you," his gaze softened for a fraction of a second when he looked at her before it hardened again. His next words came out low and threatening.

"If you want to keep your job, you better have a reasonable explanation, one which I can't wait to hear after you clean up this mess." Kyle stepped back, anger and disappointment everywhere on his face, then left the room, not even stopping when Lucas called to him.

Harmony pressed a hand to her forehead. Why, oh, why hadn't she gone to find him when she first saw the mess in his office? That would have saved everyone the trouble. Harmony had a sinking feeling in her gut when she thought about the look on Kyle's face when he saw the state of his office. Why did Kyle do that to her? He always went way overboard whenever she was involved. And could she really blame him? *Oh, Lord. Help me to make this right.*

Kyle could not believe the state of his office. He couldn't believe the gravity of his reaction or the threats he'd made. Kyle stopped in the hallway and leaned against the wall, pinching the bridge of his nose with his thumb and forefinger. He'd really gone off the deep end this time. He couldn't help himself. He'd gone into his office to get something for Lucas, and bam! He walks in to find some of his papers in shreds, others strewn across his desk and floor and there in the midst of the chaos is Harmony, under his desk for no apparent reason.

She could be working for one of the local newspapers, even one of the global ones, looking for dirt on the marvelous Kyle Taylor. Cassandra's words from weeks ago echoed in his mind. But Harmony wouldn't do that, right? He never thought she'd trash his office either. *Slow down, Taylor. You don't know the whole story.* Kyle willed himself to believe that this was not Harmony's fault, that one always had to hear both sides of the story. What kind of story could go with an event like this? The more Kyle thought about it, the angrier he got and the more he knew he needed space. He felt like such an idiot. He'd trusted Harmony, trusted her with his daughter, with his home, with his heart.

Whoa, whoa, whoa, no way was he trusting *anyone* with his heart. Nope. It was his and his alone, and he wasn't about to share it. With anyone. Even if she had mesmerizing blue eyes that sparkled whenever she was happy.

Kyle shook his head. He couldn't trust her; she'd betrayed that trust. Betrayed him. Maybe the more he said that to himself, he might actually start believing it. Believe that Harmony was capable of doing that to him. To anyone.

Suddenly, the walls around Kyle seemed to be closing in, cutting off the oxygen supply, making his head swim and his lungs burn for fresh air. He needed to get out. Now.

Blindly, Kyle sprinted down the hallway, bumping into a very surprised Clarissa and bursting out the door into the backyard. Kyle blinked in the bright sunlight, at odds with the cold temperature. The cold air stung his cheeks and chilled his body, sending goosebumps across his skin. Kyle took a few deep gulps of air, coughing as the cold air practically froze in his lungs. If it was this cold in early October, it was sure to be a cold winter. The frozen air helped to numb the pain in his heart and cool his hot temper. Well, more like redirected it. Towards himself.

Guilt and shame flowed into him like the freezing air had his lungs, nearly crippling him. He'd threatened Harmony with her job. How could he? Sure, they disagreed sometimes, but she was good with Ellie. Basically with everyone, really. Even him, actually. Then why did he always get so mad at her? Okay, well, to be honest, he got mad at Lucas, but...

Wow.

Reality hit Kyle like a sucker punch to the gut. He didn't get mad at Harmony. He got mad at Lucas. But the funny thing was, he didn't get mad at either of them alone, only when they were together. Why was that?

Because you are falling in love with Harmony and Lucas is a threat.

Okay, that's it. Last straw. Love was an extremely strong word, one which did not suit his relationship with Harmony at all. And Lucas, a threat? Come on. There was really only one thing left to do: Kyle was going for a skate. Maybe afterwards, his office would be cleaned up and Lucas would be gone and…maybe he'd even be back in his right mind.

Chapter Seventeen

Harmony sat down on the overstuffed caramel coloured couch in the living room where they hosted the adults bible study. After Kyle had left, she and Lucas had managed to clean up the papers, throwing the shredded ones away and putting the rest in a neat pile on his desk.

Harmony couldn't help feeling more than a little bit angry at Kyle. In fact, she'd been pretty miffed at Lucas for his "straw that broke the camel's back" comment. She'd even confronted him about it.

"Why do you egg him on like that? You had to have known that what you said wasn't going to help."

Lucas had looked at her with a small smile on his face.

"We're friends, right, Harmony?" he'd asked her, ignoring her question.

She'd frowned slightly, taken aback by his question. "Of course we are."

"Do you trust me?"

Harmony had nodded, confused at the turn their conversation had taken. "Yes."

Lucas had smiled, and then gone back to picking up pieces of shredded pages. "Good."

Now she was more confused than ever. She had no clue what was going on with Lucas and all his cryptic comments, and she was still mad at Kyle. She'd been angry at him all afternoon and well into the evening. Even Ellie had noticed that she was a little off. Harmony hadn't even felt like going to bible study that evening, and that's when she knew she really needed to. She'd been making a concentrated effort to see the whole ordeal from Kyle's perspective. Granted, she was certain that if it had been her office, and Lucas had said what he did to Kyle to her, she would have been pretty mad. Angry. Enraged. *Oh, Lord,* Harmony prayed, *please don't let me lose my job for this.*

Harmony didn't know what she would do if she lost this job. She loved Ellie with all her heart, and being here with Lily and Marjorie, she felt like she was a part of a family again. Aside from that, she'd left her whole life behind in Indonesia, but she didn't think that God was calling her back into missions. If she lost this job, she didn't know what she'd do.

Harmony redirected her thoughts towards how glad she was that Lily had decided to give bible study a try. Lily hadn't been very open to the idea at first, and Harmony had honestly been very surprised to see her show up. When she wasn't working at the spa in the fancy hotel downtown, Lily spent a lot of her free time looking for a site to reopen her own spa business, but so far, she hadn't found anything she could afford.

Just then Pastor Martin Schmidt called them to attention and opened in a word of prayer, pulling Harmony from her thoughts.

Harmony could feel the tension easing from her shoulders and her muscles slowly relaxing. She loved worshiping God with other people at church, at prayer meeting, at choir, anywhere. Most of all, she loved worshiping with her own people, in her own language, and with her own church. This was something she hadn't known she was missing when she'd grown up in Indonesia. She'd only been seven when her parents moved their family overseas. She wasn't sure what it was, but something about worshiping with other Canadians made it a little bit more meaningful. Special. Whatever the reason, Harmony felt blessed to be here.

Pastor Schmidt sat in the front of the room, by the stone fireplace where the flames were dancing and jumping merrily, as if they themselves were worshiping God. As the lesson wore on, Harmony started fidgeting in her chair. His study was on forgiveness. Even if someone didn't ask and didn't even deserve it, as Christians, we were called to forgive. The scripture he chose was Matthew 18:21-22 which read: "Then Peter came to Jesus and asked, 'Lord, how many times shall I forgive my brother when he sins against me? Up to seven times?' Jesus answered, 'I tell you, not seven times, but seventy-seven times.'"

Forgive.

Unconditionally.

Harmony sighed. Forgiveness was not one of her strong points. It was hard to remember, but she might be the only living bible Kyle would ever read. Whatever she did, she would impact the lives around her and their views on Christianity. On Christ. Would she be the turning point? And which way would they turn?

Harmony closed her eyes, bowing her head and silently praying. For wisdom. For grace.

Oh, Lord. Help me, she prayed. *Lord, I want to be a light in this family. I want You to reign in this place. In their hearts and in mine.* Harmony sighed, trying to hold back the tears that stung the back of her eyes. *I love you, Lord. Let that love shine.* Harmony raised her face and opened her eyes.

She knew what she was going to do. After bible study, she would go and ask Kyle for forgiveness and she would explain to him what had happened. Her blue eyes were swimming with unshed tears. But they were those wonderful, loving, hurting tears that she was sure were sent from God. They were the kind of tears that didn't make you sad but relieved. Awed. Harmony tuned in to the pastor's sermon just as he said something that was like an arrow to the heart.

"The thing is, God doesn't just want you to forgive others. He wants you to forgive yourself. You can't live in the victory of Christ if you are living under the bondage of guilt. You just can't."

Harmony felt like she was choking. Forgiving others she could manage. But forgiving herself? For letting Roger die? Not so much. *It wasn't your fault.* Harmony almost felt as if she could hear the Holy Spirit whispering to her soul. But that was weird, right? I mean, the Holy Spirit only spoke to righteous people. *There was nothing you could have done.* Wasn't there? Hadn't there been some way that she could have prevented his untimely death? *No.*

Harmony nearly gasped as the truth resonated with her soul. There hadn't been anything that she could have done to save Roger. His death wasn't her fault. Harmony's breath caught in her throat.

She didn't need to forgive herself. She shouldn't have been angry with herself in the first place. With that realization Harmony felt...joyful...at peace. She wanted to jump, dance, and shout praises to the Lord for setting her free. And she was free indeed.

Harmony got up quietly out of her seat and walked through the kitchen to the backdoor. She burst out the door and took a few quick breaths of the cold air. Harmony felt overwhelmed but in a good way by the love of God. She felt like she was caught up in an avalanche of God's love and forgiveness. Forgiveness. The word echoed in her mind and reverberated in her soul.

"Oh, God," Harmony prayed. "Thank you."

A sound behind her caused her to turn around. Kyle had skated over to the edge of the skating rink, coming to a stop as close to where she was standing as possible and wearing a very annoyed expression. Harmony could feel her anger creeping up but stopped it with a single thought. *Forgiveness.* Harmony sighed and realized that when she looked closely, Kyle wasn't only annoyed. He was hurt. She frowned slightly, wondering if he'd been skating out here since the whole fiasco in the office. Compassion for Kyle softened her heart towards him and cooled whatever remained of her anger.

"Kyle," Harmony flinched and smoothed back her hair. She sounded pathetic, even to herself. "I, um, I just wanted to say that I'm sorry about the state of your office and," Harmony took a step forward and met Kyle's intense stare. "I was looking for Mookie because he was missing, and the way you saw your office when you came in was the way that I found it. I had almost caught Mookie when you came in."

Kyle looked away from her and shifted from foot to foot, skate to skate. Harmony continued despite his feigned disinterest.

"Kyle, no ferret could have done all that. I only know that despite what you probably think, I didn't trash your office and it would be impossible for Mookie to have done so."

Kyle only crossed his arms over his broad chest and stared at the ice at his feet as if he hadn't heard her. Harmony felt her hurt and annoyance rising in her throat like bile. She clamped her lips shut and turned around abruptly, her head held high even though her heart felt as if it had just been run over by a stampede of horses. Or maybe just a couple of skates.

*****

"So, what's going on between you and my brother?"

Harmony looked over her shoulder to meet Lily's inquiring brown eyes.

"What do you mean?" Harmony replied innocently, trying to avoid the question as she wandered through the house. Marjorie was in the kitchen with Clarissa. Ellie was already asleep and Kyle was at a hockey club meeting. Kyle and Harmony had been ignoring each other for the past week since the office incident. It had made things at home a lot more strained. Lily rolled her eyes and arched one of her perfectly plucked eyebrows.

"Are you kidding me? You guys have been going around, pretending that the other isn't even there, for like, the past week or something. What's up?"

Harmony sighed and turned towards Lily.

"Your brother and I have had a bit of a...misunderstanding, that's all. Besides, it will blow over and this will all be behind us. No cause for worry."

Lily snorted. "And when exactly will it blow over? Next week? Or maybe next month? Come on, Harmony. You two can't still be mad about that messy office thing, can you?"

Harmony wasn't about to continue this conversation.

"Look, Lily," her voice came out much sharper than she intended, but she went on anyway. "It's over and done, so can you get off my back about it?" Harmony turned abruptly and grabbed the book that she'd left on the counter that morning, showing with her body language that the conversation was over. Lily brushed past her in a huff and sauntered over to the sofa in front of the TV, turning it on with a flick of her wrist on the remote.

Out of the corner of her eye, Harmony saw Lily's back go ramrod straight and heard the agonized "oh no" escape her lips. Harmony looked up and saw Lily holding her hand over her mouth, her shoulders shaking from her silent sobs. Harmony looked at the TV and felt her heart lurch to her throat. A wave of nausea hit her, and for a moment, the room spun and tilted before abruptly righting itself and coming to a stop, her vision zooming in on the TV. Marjorie walked cheerfully into the room, unaware of the intensity of the situation.

"Is the PVR working? I set it to tape the news again, but last time, it didn't work…" Her voice died off when she saw the headlines floating across the top of the TV. SPORTS CAR HIT BY SEMI.

There was dead silence in the room as images of the scene flashed across the screen. Images of the debris of a destroyed sports car. Of a red sports car. Kyle owned a red sports car, a bright red Lamborghini. But it couldn't be his, could it? No, his sports car had the license plate: TAYLOR.

The thought flashed through Harmony's brain just as a picture of the back of the sports car showed the license plate: TAYLOR. The front of the car was wedged under the semi, completely destroyed, looking as if someone had crumpled the it. The accident happened on the same route Kyle took to and from the rink.

Oh, Lord. Please don't let it be true. The words went around and around in Harmony's head, identical to the news headlines on TV. She could hear the voice of the anchorman droning in the background of her thoughts. "As you can see, the front of the car is completely destroyed… One man has been taken to the hospital with only minor injuries but is now unconscious…authorities are still trying to determine the cause of the accident…"

Harmony was almost sick with worry. She could see the pictures and there was no way anyone or anything could have survived the wreckage. The only person who could go away with only minor injuries was the driver of the semi which meant… Harmony felt as if the air had been sucked out of her lungs. She couldn't lose him. She didn't think she would survive if anything happened to him.

Chapter Eighteen

Kyle got up out of Lucas' sleek Porsche pulling his duffle bag out with him.

"Thanks for the ride, man."

Lucas nodded to him, starting up the engine. "No problem."

Lucas always took the long way whenever he drove from the rink to Kyle's place. Kyle really didn't understand why Lucas didn't just go take the more direct route the way Kyle did, but hey, he wasn't about to become a backseat driver; he was just grateful for the ride. Kyle walked up to the house, surprised to find it in complete darkness. He figured that Ellie was asleep, but usually Marjorie, Lily, and Harmony stayed up and talked about "girl stuff" late into the night. He sighed as he thought of Harmony.

He hated to think that Cassandra was right about Harmony, that she would try to place the blame on someone else even when she was caught red handed. Yet he couldn't help but believe Harmony when she said that she didn't trash his office. And granted it was pretty unlikely that a little ferret could wreak so much havoc. But then, if Harmony didn't do it, who did? He'd just have to be more careful and keep an eye on her. That wouldn't be so hard since she lived with him, and honestly, Harmony was pretty easy on the eyes. Kyle unlocked the front door and entered, surprised again to hear no merry chatter. Weird.

"Hello?" Kyle called down the dark hallway, the only light coming from what looked like the family room fireplace and maybe the TV. Kyle flicked on the hall light and made his way towards the family room. He came in, surprised that no one appeared to have heard his voice. He leaned against the arch doorway, glancing quickly at the

TV then at the depressed, morbid faces watching it. Must be some sad romantic chick flick.

"Hey, guys," Kyle greeted them. "What's up?"

All heads in the room turned and stared at him for one tense moment before all three women pitched themselves into his arms. Kyle stumbled and nearly fell, and only regained his balance thanks to the sturdy wall beside him. There was a tidal wave of choked voices saying things like,

"You're all right," "we were so worried," and then, "I love you so much."

That, of course, was his mother speaking, though Kyle could not understand what the fuss was about. It was just hockey practice. Suddenly, his mother moved and sat slowly on the couch, sobbing, and Lily rushed over to comfort her. In the blink of an eye, it was just Harmony nestled in his arms. She raised her face and looked up at him, her eyes swimming with tears. Kyle had the strangest urge to kiss her, to kiss her until she forgot whatever it was that had brought tears to her eyes. He just might have, had not his sister interrupted him.

"Kyle, what happened out there?"

Kyle looked up and reluctantly let go of Harmony, not liking the cold feeling of something missing when she wasn't in his arms. He felt as if he'd just lost something special, something important. He tore his gaze away from her and looked at his sister.

"What are you talking about?"

Marjorie looked up and pointed at the TV screen, unable to speak through her tears. Kyle grabbed the remote, rewound the program until the beginning, and watched in amazement as the story unfolded. Or in this case, the news report. When it finished, Kyle looked around the room and sat down near his mother, putting his arm around her shoulders.

"Well," he began, "that is definitely my car, but I had no idea this had happened. Lucas gave me a ride home and he likes to go the long way, so we missed that accident completely. There was something wrong with the transmission, so I had it towed at the end of practice."

Kyle reached up and rubbed the back of his neck. "I should call the tow truck company and make sure that the driver is all right."

Lily came and sat down beside him, and Harmony sat on the other side of Marjorie. Lily grabbed his hand and laid her head on his shoulder.

"I'm just glad you're all right," she whispered softly. Kyle was glad he was all right too. Kyle looked around and realized that someone was missing.

"Where's Ellie?" He couldn't bear to think that she was scared and wondering if her daddy was alive when everyone else knew that he was fine. Harmony glanced up and motioned to the second floor.

"She was in bed before we found out, and we didn't want to worry her before we knew for sure. She should still be asleep."

Kyle nodded and got up, assuring his mother that he was fine and that they should all go get some sleep. Kyle entered his daughter's room to find Ellie fast asleep, surrounded in pink and holding the disastrous ferret Mookie in her arms. He leaned over and kissed her forehead, smoothing her hair away from her face. Out of the corner of his eye, he noticed a shadow pass through the light of the doorway, and he turned around to find Harmony, peeking in through the opened door. Kyle quietly exited the room and met her in the hallway.

"The tow truck driver is fine, same with the driver of the semi, only minor injuries." He thought she'd probably like to know.

"Are *you* okay?" He asked stepping just a little bit closer. She looked up at him, her blue eyes sparkling in the dim hallway and shallow lighting.

"I'm just glad you're safe." Her voice was barely above a whisper, and it seemed to float towards him like a soft summer breeze. She ducked her head momentarily before raising her eyes to meet his again. "I'm sorry about everything that's been going on this week, what with the office and—"

"Shhh, Harmony. It's fine." Kyle placed his hands on her shoulders and looked straight into her eyes. "It's all forgotten, okay?"

Harmony nodded. "I just, I don't know what we would have done if anything happened to you," she continued softly, and Kyle reluctantly let his hands drop from her shoulders. Harmony glanced through the partially open door, no doubt looking at the little girl situated in an overflow of pink blankets and cushions. "What *she* would have done without you."

Kyle turned and looked into Harmony's blue eyes and raised his hand to cup her cheek.

"At least she would have had you." Kyle's voice came out in a harsh whisper, choked with emotions that he didn't want to identify. Harmony leaned into him, only slightly, just enough to let him know that what she said next was true.

"She'll always need her daddy."

Kyle couldn't help but think about how beautiful Harmony was, how kind, honest, wise, and sweet. And then he couldn't help but think about how much he...cared for her. The depth of his feelings for her scared him more than he cared to admit.

On top of that, she was his employee, his daughter's nanny. Could they ever have a shot at a real relationship? Kyle had the sinking feeling that they couldn't. Besides, she didn't feel the same way about him. Did she? Kyle dropped his hand and took a step back.

"Good night, Harmony." He watched her turn and walk to her room, all the while feeling like she had taken his heart with her.

*****

Kyle ripped his gaze away from Harmony in order to focus on the princess movie that all four women (including Ellie) had forced him to watch. Unfortunately, the women of the house outnumbered him four to one. But somehow, though it was a real shocker, he couldn't stay focused on the movie. Harmony was sitting just out of arms reach, beside Ellie who sat snuggled up to him. Lily was laying on the love seat and Marjorie occupied the armchair. Lily and Ellie had just gotten up to get some snacks when the phone rang.

Kyle snatched the phone out of its cradle and checked the call display. He could almost feel his heart land in his stomach.

"Mom, it's for you." Kyle sounded gruff and harsh, maybe afraid, even to himself.

Marjorie took the phone warily and walked over to a far corner in the room in order to speak in private. Kyle tried to clamp down on the feelings of dread that were creeping up inside of him. He'd recognized the number instantly. It was from the cancer clinic, and Kyle couldn't help but be worried. Had they found something on her routine CT scan last week? What if Marjorie's cancer had come back? What if it had spread? What if it was terminal? What would he do without his mom? Kyle couldn't bear to contemplate the thought.

As he gazed at his mother's face, wanting to gauge her reaction, his fears increased and his throat tightened. His mother's face blanched, then she set her chin determinedly as she slowly nodded and hung up the phone.

Kyle opened his mouth to ask her about it when she quickly shook her head, giving him a brave smile. Kyle suddenly felt as though the weight of the world had been placed on his shoulders. Kyle let his head drop into his hand, stifling a groan. He couldn't lose his mother, not now. Kyle turned when he felt a hand on his shoulder. Harmony's eyes were warm and understanding, and they reflected the same fears that were no doubt evident in his own eyes. Somehow, it was comforting to know that someone else knew exactly how he felt, without him ever having to say a thing. He felt even better, knowing that that person was Harmony.

Lily and Ellie reentered the room, stopping him from asking his mother about the phone call outright. He glanced back at Harmony, finding it strangely comforting to think that, though he would definitely not consider himself at all religious, knowing that she was probably praying for him and his mother right this minute nearly made his day.

Chapter Nineteen

Harmony dried Ellie off with a little pink towel after their swim in the pool. The joys of having an indoor pool. Considering that at the moment it was snowing outside Harmony was extremely glad of that fact.

Harmony did, however, have a nagging feeling that something was wrong in this house. Even Ellie's merry chatter didn't ease the queasy feeling in her stomach. It wasn't anything really noticeable; no dark cloud of sorrow had descended upon the household. It was just a feeling that Harmony had in the pit of her stomach.

Harmony thought back to the day that Marjorie received that phone call. Marjorie hadn't changed, at least not drastically. She'd been distracted lately, but she continued to be her good natured, doting self. Truth be told, it wasn't really Marjorie Harmony was worried about. It was Kyle.

Whatever assumptions she had on Marjorie's health, she had gleaned from Kyle's demeanor. Harmony knew that Marjorie had had a bout with cancer and had been recovering from a mastectomy and chemotherapy around the time Ellie was born. Though she was worried about Marjorie's health, she knew that Marjorie's faith would carry her through whatever the days ahead may bring.

Kyle didn't have anything to sustain him. He had little understanding of what Christ had done for him, and he definitely wasn't about to trust God with his problems, especially not when it came to his mother. And Harmony completely understood his worry. But she also knew that God had a greater plan than any of them could hope to imagine. It didn't necessarily make the trials hurt any less, but it was comforting to know that God had a plan. Harmony only wished that Kyle could understand that.

"Miss Hawmony?" Ellie's sweet little voice pulled her from her thoughts and caused Harmony to paste a smile on her face and turned to the child, trying to push her tumultuous thoughts aside. Harmony knelt down to Ellie's height so that they were looking each other in the eye.

"Yes, honey?"

Ellie's eyes narrowed, her brows met in a confused, inquisitive V, and her lips puckered as she asked, "What's wrong wit Gwammy?"

Harmony felt her smile fading but she quickly recovered, fighting to keep her voice even and calm.

"What do you mean, Ellie?"

Best to find out how much the little girl knew and how much she had overheard before scaring her over something that Harmony herself wasn't sure about. Ellie shrugged one of her small shoulders as she pulled her pink T-shirt over her head.

"Gwammy seems diffwent, and Daddy is always wit her *all* de time. I just tought someting was wrong."

Harmony breathed a sigh of relief as she helped Ellie slip into her beige cords and her fuzzy pink slippers. "I'm sure everything's fine, so don't worry, okay?"

"I'm not wowied." Ellie grinned up at her, her brown eyes twinkling. "God's got a pwan."

Harmony gaped after her, a slow smile stretching across her lips as she watched Ellie skip away towards the kitchen, no doubt having smelt the chocolate chip cookies Clarissa had planned on baking. Out of the mouth of babes. Harmony shook her head in disbelief, wondering at how trusting that Ellie was, knowing that her God was in control and that no matter what, God loved her and wanted what was best for her. Maybe that was why God wanted His followers to have childlike faith. Faith that would trust that their Father loved them and would not let anything bad happen to them. Yes, God's got a plan, and it's a perfect, beautiful plan.

Harmony sighed, praying once again that Kyle would come to trust God with everything. Even with his life.

*****

Marjorie was in the family room, and thankfully, she was alone. That would no doubt make the following conversation easier on her, since Kyle wasn't going to leave her alone until he had answers. Kyle cleared his throat, alerting Marjorie of his presence so as not to startle her.

"Hey, Mom." He came over and stood beside her, as she gazed through the window and onto the happy scene of Harmony and Ellie building a very tall, strange-looking snowman.

"Look at them," Marjorie whispered as she smiled wistfully. "Look at how happy Ellie is with Harmony, how much more talkative she is. You definitely made the right decision in hiring her." His mother's face was calm, and she had a peace about her that unnerved him. Yet at the same time, he desperately wished to have that peace.

"Well, actually," he said, wrapping his arms around her and resting his chin on the top of her head, "you hired her."

Marjorie chuckled. "Kids grow up so fast," she whispered. "Ellie will be four in May." Marjorie frowned slightly. "I just hope I'm around to see her birthday."

"Don't talk like that, Mom, please," Kyle begged. "What's going on? Please tell me what's wrong. I can't help you unless I know what we're up against." Kyle's heart took a beating as he waited for her to continue.

Stepping away from him, Marjorie turned away from the window and smiled at him encouragingly, though her eyes became misty. She squeezed his hands tightly.

"Kyle, honey, I don't want you to worry, but the doctor seems to think that the cancer's come back and—"

"You don't want me to worry?" Kyle asked incredulously. "Mom, how can you be so calm about this?" Kyle pinched the bridge of his nose, battling back the migraine that he felt coming on. Kyle sighed and sank into the nearest sofa.

"How…how do they know it's cancer?" Kyle could feel the cold hand of dread wrapping its icy fingers around his heart, making it difficult to breathe, even to think. This couldn't be happening. His mom couldn't get cancer again. Not again.

"They saw something on my CT scan and they want me to come in for an ultrasound on Tuesday," Marjorie said it matter-of-factly, the same way she would say that Clarissa had forgotten to buy milk at the grocery store.

Kyle hated the helplessness he felt, unable to do anything to fix this or to help his mother.

Marjorie laid a hand on Kyle's shoulder in an attempt to comfort him. It wasn't working.

"Mom, don't worry. We'll figure this out. I can take you to the check up and everything." Kyle ran his fingers through his thick brown hair and sighed, summoning all the strength he could muster just to get the words out. "We beat this once. we'll beat it again."

They had to. If he lost his mother now... No, that wasn't going to happen. He wouldn't let it happen. He would move heaven and earth to keep her healthy. Kyle knew that he wasn't ready to let her go, and part of him didn't think he ever would be. Kyle forced his accelerated heartbeat to slow as he stood and pulled Marjorie into his arms.

"Kyle," Marjorie leaned back to look up at him and raised a hand to touch his cheek. "I'm not worried. Jesus said, 'Therefore, do not worry about tomorrow, for tomorrow will worry about its own things. Sufficient for the day is its own trouble.'" Marjorie stared straight into Kyle's eyes, making sure that he was listening to her. "God has a good plan for my life, and I trust Him to do what is best for me, no matter what that may be."

For a split second, Kyle wished that he had faith like his mother's or Harmony's. He wished he believed that God really cared about what was going on in his life. Kyle let go of Marjorie and rubbed the back of his neck, trying to process everything he'd just learned. Trying to sort out all that he had to do.

"Mom... I don't think you should tell Lily yet, not until you've had the test and we have the results back. No need to worry her." Or deal with all the drama that would come with her knowing. Lily hadn't taken the cancer very well the first time around, and there was no reason to borrow trouble before they knew anything for certain.

"You know what, honey? I think I'm going to go lie down for a little while. It's been a long day."

Kyle watched as Marjorie left the room, looking just as strong and independent as she always did. How did she do it?

Kyle dropped down onto the couch, staring into space and feeling like a part of him had just been ripped out. What was he supposed to do without his mom? What were any of them going to do if they lost her? Kyle felt the strongest desire to have someone to confide in. Someone who would understand. Someone who would make his sorrows less intense and his joys more immense. Someone who would be his helper, his partner, and his friend.

Almost uncontrollably, Kyle found his gaze pulled towards the big picture window and to the white world beyond. Harmony and Ellie had completed their snowman, adding arms, a scarf, and… his old hockey helmet? Despite the sadness of what Marjorie had just revealed to him, Kyle found himself laughing, especially when they added a beat-up old hockey stick. They were making a snow*dad* instead of just a plain old snow*man*.

Harmony glanced up and saw him through the window and waved. She was so beautiful, especially when she smiled like that. Kyle felt his stomach bunch up with longing. That was the way it should always be: him, Ellie, and Harmony as a family. The trouble wouldn't be convincing Ellie, but convincing Harmony.

Kyle was pulled from his daydream of family and love by the ice-cold reality check that might mean losing his mother. Kyle could feel the claustrophobic feeling coming on, like whenever he was stressed or afraid, and he felt the urge to go outside to escape. Kyle honestly couldn't think of what to do or where to go, but he needed to breathe and clear his head. He needed to suck it up, buckle down, and pull himself together. Because Marjorie needed him now, more than ever.

Chapter Twenty

Harmony laughed as she pulled snow from Ellie's damp hair. This was an extremely difficult task, since Ellie insisted upon giggling and bouncing around like crazy. After what must have been at least fifteen minutes, Harmony finally had the little girl out of her snowsuit and into a clean pair of comfy pink sweatpants. Harmony sent her off to the living room to grab some coloring books and such so that she would have time to get out of her own heavy, wet snowsuit.

Harmony entered the living room where Ellie was playing and happened to glance out the window towards their snowman. It really was a very comical snowman. Armed with a helmet and a hockey stick, it was the spitting image of Kyle. Harmony's heart skipped a beat. Well, not exactly like Kyle.

Harmony's mind flashed back to that night when they'd thought he had been in the car accident. When he'd touched her cheek... Harmony shook her head as if to ward off wayward thoughts. Harmony and Kyle didn't have a future. He wasn't a Christian, and she knew what God's Word said about being yoked with a nonbeliever. "Do not be bound together with unbelievers; for what partnership have righteousness and lawlessness, or what fellowship has light with darkness" (2 Corinthians 6:14)? Harmony had never thought that that particular verse would ever apply to her, and she'd never thought that following it would be so hard.

Then again, she had never encountered anyone like Kyle before. He was so different. He was such a complicated arrangement of conflicting characters but such an enticing person. If she wasn't careful, she'd end up losing her heart to him, and that was one thing she could not afford to lose. She just hoped it wasn't already too late.

Harmony's eyes drifted over to the skating rink where she could see just one end of the rink and one of the two benches on either side of it. She saw Kyle sitting on the bench with his back to her, his shoulders slumped forward and his forearms resting on his knees. She couldn't tell from this distance for sure, but she could judge by his posture that he was sad. Concerned. Afraid.

Harmony felt her heart lurch with the desire to comfort him. To share his burden. She knew what it was like to have something bunched up inside, screaming to be let out and shared, making whoever carried it absolutely miserable. Not that she'd learned much from it, considering that she'd never told anyone about what had actually happened to Roger. Harmony noticed a person approaching from the corner of her eye and was pulled from her thoughts by Lily's voice.

"He looks totally depressed," she stated smoothly, obviously unconcerned. "He could probably use a friend right about now," she added with a wink at Harmony. Pausing, Lily's brows furrowed as she thought about it. "It can't be that serious."

Harmony wasn't so sure. She had suspicions about Marjorie's condition, but she didn't want to worry her friend. "Why don't you go talk to him?" Harmony asked, not quite sure what Lily's motives were for this smooth my-brother-really-needs-a-friend speech. Lily just rolled her eyes.

"I said he needed a *friend,* someone to comfort him, not someone to help him start World War Three."

It was Harmony's turn to roll her eyes. Lily and Kyle did argue and bicker, but they were always there when either of them needed support. Kyle had even leased a building downtown and was having someone fix it up as a surprise present for Lily. Harmony had been honored that he had chosen to share that information with her. Meanwhile, Lily was working as assistant manager at a hotel salon. Lily gave Harmony a friendly shove towards the hallway leading to the backdoor.

"Go talk to Kyle. I'll take Miss Ellie and we'll go bake some cookies and have some hot chocolate."

Ellie, who had been coloring silently and completely oblivious only minutes ago, now had her full attention focused on Lily.

"We can bake cookies?" she asked, almost as if it was too good to be true. Harmony realized with a smidgen of remorse that she and Ellie hadn't done any baking together if Clarissa wasn't around, partly because Harmony really couldn't cook or bake and partly because she didn't know that Ellie would even be interested.

"Of course, sweetheart," Lily chimed, tweaking the little girl's nose.

"All right, I will be back soon," Harmony said, walking towards the backdoor. Then she turned around and winked, saying, "Just in time to eat all the cookies."

Girlish laughter followed her as she exited the room. When she opened the backdoor, a blast of icy air nearly stole the breath from her lungs. Harmony shivered, wishing she had grabbed a sweater or maybe even a jacket. Alberta weather was notoriously unpredictable, and when she had been outside playing with Ellie only moments ago, it had been chilly but not uncomfortably so. The previously mild day was now exceedingly cold, and she wished she had thought to check the electronic thermometer. She shivered again, wrapping her arms around her as she made her way through the ankle-high snow, marveling at what a cold late October day it was turning out to be.

As Harmony approached the bench where Kyle sat, slumped over and staring off into space, her heart went out to him, and she prayed that God would give her the wisdom and the compassion to help. And the strength to guard her heart.

Harmony sat down beside him, staying silent for a moment with her arms crossed over her chest for warmth. She could only imagine how cold Kyle was; she'd only been outside for a moment and her feet and fingers were already going numb. After another moment of silence, Harmony asked the question she hoped she wouldn't have to ever ask, given her growing love and respect for Marjorie and her family.

"Is it your mom?"

Kyle still didn't make eye contact but kept staring into the distance, and he nodded.

Harmony blew out a breath and sighed. "Does it have anything to do with the phone call she received the other day?" Harmony dreaded the answer he was surely about to give her and held her breath, hoping, praying…

"They think Mom has cancer again."

Harmony felt the whoosh of the air leaving her lungs, as though the news punched her in the stomach.

Kyle ran his fingers through his thick brown hair and sighed. "They know they got all of it with the surgery, but they think it may have spread and gone undetected before then. Something showed up on a routine CT scan, and they think it's cancer. Again."

Harmony could hear the bitterness in his voice. She could see the confusion in his intense brown eyes.

"Oh, Kyle. I'm so sorry," she said, reaching out and taking his hand in hers. She paused for a minute before adding, "Do you want me to pray for you?"

Kyle withdrew his hand and shook his head. "As if that would do any good. You shouldn't waste your breath." His voice was laced with bitterness and anger, along with something else: fear. Kyle Taylor was afraid. Afraid of trusting God, afraid of losing someone he loved.

"Kyle, how can you say that? God loves you and he cares about what's going on in your life and with the people you love."

Kyle shook his head, his intense brown eyes raising to meet hers. "That's a nice thought. But the reality is, (a) God has favourites, (b) God doesn't care, (c) God's not listening, or (d) all of the above."

Harmony sat stunned, finding her heart filled with compassion and praying that the Holy Spirit would guide her and give her the right words to say. She cocked her head to one side and *really* looked at him, because behind those angry brown eyes was a world of pain and hurt.

"And how did you come to those conclusions, Kyle?" Harmony asked, keeping her voice calm. "Because God doesn't answer all your prayers? God's not a vending machine, Kyle. You can't just put your prayer quarter in and out pops whatever you asked for. That's not the way God works."

Kyle didn't answer. He just sat, rubbing his hands together. His face was pensive and guarded, but at least he hadn't stormed off and left her alone on the bench. Harmony paused, looking for another analogy that would make sense to him.

"Can you see the future, Kyle?" When he didn't say anything, she continued on, her heart sinking with the feeling that she failed. She wasn't getting through. She wasn't a very good witness. Harmony shook off those thoughts, praying for some type of reaction, acknowledgement, anything.

"Don't you think that God must care? He sees the big picture, how what happens today influences tomorrow. We don't." Harmony sighed, shivering. "You yourself are living proof that God cares and that he has a plan for our lives. Your car was totaled and had it not broken down and you had not needed to get a ride from Lucas, you could have been in it. The Bible talks about this in Jeremiah 29:11: 'For I know the plans that I have for you,' declares the Lord, 'plans for welfare and not for calamity, to give you a future and a hope.'"

Kyle turned to her and asked a question she was neither expecting nor prepared to answer at first. "Your fiancé died in the mission field. How did serving God give him either a future or a hope? How has it given you and future and a hope?"

Harmony swallowed hard. She had been battling with the same doubts for almost a year.

"Once you've accepted Christ, you know that you will not walk through any of life's struggles alone and that you will go to heaven when you die. That was his future, his hope, and now, it's his present. My future on earth is in God's hands, but my everlasting hope is that I will see Roger once again, and that I will see my God face-to-face. That's what I believe, and that's what I know is true."

Kyle looked at her for a minute and then he leaned back on the bench, considering what she had said. Harmony knew it was all up to the Holy Spirit, but she was sort of hoping for an all-out conversion to Christianity there and then. *Any personal reasons for that wish?* Okay, no. She had no reason for wanting Kyle to become a Christian aside from the fact that she wanted everyone to be saved. Yeah, right. Harmony shivered again and Kyle glanced her way.

123

"You cold?"

How did the man manage to say the simplest thing and nearly make her lose her head? Harmony smiled sheepishly.

"Maybe a little bit," she admitted quietly, not really wanting to draw so much attention to herself, even though it was just Kyle and herself alone on the bench. Before she could analyze the feelings he evoked, Kyle wrapped his arm around her and rubbed his hand up and down her arm. Harmony turned to look him in the eye, and as their eyes met, she felt a wave of awareness smash into her, making her wonder if she was falling in love with Kyle. She couldn't; that wouldn't be right. She could think of a million reasons why a relationship with Kyle would never work, most importantly the fact that they didn't operate on the same belief system and that he was her boss. But at that very moment, the reasons didn't matter one bit. Was there no chance for them? Kyle's hand stopped and rested on her upper arm, his dark eyes gazing into hers. All Harmony could think about was what it would be like to have him kiss her. She inhaled sharply and stood up. She had to stop thinking things like that.

"We, uh, I should get back to Ellie and Lily. They were baking cookies." Harmony smoothed a lock of her hair behind her ear and resisted the urge to shiver again, feeling colder than she had before, now that Kyle's arm was not around her. The verse 2 Corinthians 6:14 came to mind again, and Harmony steeled her resolve and took another step away from Kyle, both physically and emotionally, fearing that if she let him into her heart, she would never let him out. As she turned to go, Kyle called to her.

"Hey, Harmony. Please don't tell Lily about what's going on with Mom. It might be nothing, and we don't want to worry her."

Harmony nodded her consent before turning back to the house and walking as fast as she could without being too obvious. She couldn't let herself fall for Kyle. She just couldn't. She was worried that if she fell for him, she would never have the strength to get back up.

Chapter Twenty-One

Kyle pondered Harmony's words for the rest of the weekend. He couldn't get them out of his head. Or the way she fit perfectly in the crook of his arm. Or how beautiful she looked against the white snowy backdrop. But that was beside the point.

What she had said about God and them not seeing the big picture made sense. Perfect sense. And yet, Kyle couldn't let go of all the times God had let him down. All the times God had seemed to be against him. Had He been? A few days ago, Kyle's answer would have been a definite yes. Now, he wasn't so sure. What if God did care? What if it was true that God loved them, that God loved him? Well, there was only one way to find out.

Kyle turned over in bed and sighed. It wasn't really all that early, but he liked to sleep in on Sundays when he didn't have hockey practice or a game to get ready for. Still, something in what Harmony said made him curious. And besides, it would give him ample time to spend with his daughter. He was actually building a relationship with her, and he wanted to get to know her even better and just be there for her.

Kyle somehow managed to get groomed and dressed in taupe pants and blazer with a forest-green dress shirt. Kyle got into the rental car he'd been driving since the accident, and pulled out of the driveway. Everyone else had already left for their Sunday school classes, but Kyle hadn't seen any point in going for that. He managed to find his way to the church in the nick of time and entered the sanctuary feeling a little bit uncomfortable when he thought about all the church services he'd been to before. It had mostly consisted of Christmas Eve services and such, since his mother had only become a Christian a short time before he went away to play minor league hockey. He hadn't been to church since.

Kyle felt his phone buzz and glanced at the screen before turning it off. No way was he answering. It was Cassandra calling him again. She called him all the time. Literally.

Kyle scanned the pews and saw his mother, Harmony, Ellie, Lily, and… Lucas? Since when did Lucas come to this church? To any church? Kyle clamped down the irrational surge of jealousy at seeing Lucas sitting all close to Harmony and made his way down the aisle. He tapped Marjorie on the shoulder and she scooted to the end of the pew, giving him space to sit down. Right next to Harmony. Kyle couldn't comprehend the sudden nervousness that overcame him, especially when Harmony looked up at him with surprise and delight brightening her features. Ellie was sitting on her lap, and when she noticed him, she smiled a wide toothy grin.

"Daddy! You came!" she said, crawling onto his lap. Kyle sighed as she cuddled up against him, trying to focus on making his daughter happy and the upcoming sermon instead of on what a ridiculous flirt Lucas was. The guy had no tact. This was a church, for Pete's sake! Kyle tried, really he did, not to take too much pleasure in the fact that Harmony was clearly uncomfortable with the whole situation.

Kyle sighed again, cradling Ellie in his arms as he wondered what on earth he would do about everything that was going on. He had so much on his plate and so many what-ifs to deal with. What if his mom had cancer? What if something happened to her? What would he do without her? What would Ellie do? Or Lily? And what if he gave this Christianity thing a shot and just ended up more hurt and confused than before?

Marjorie nudged him, stirring him from his depressing thoughts as Pastor Schmidt took the pulpit. Kyle stiffened as Lucas leaned over and whispered something in Harmony's ear and scooted just a bit closer on the pew. Lily, who was sitting on the other side of Lucas, leaned over to grab a hymnal. She also scooted just a little bit closer. Harmony, looking wide-eyed and a bit confused, moved a little bit closer to him.

Kyle liked the fact that she moved further away from Lucas and closer and closer to him. The more Lily flirted with Lucas, the more Lucas flirted with Harmony and the closer Harmony moved towards him, until everyone was squished onto a quarter of the pew when they could have taken up more than half. Marjorie threw some angry looks at the two at the end of the pew. She leaned over and whispered harshly, "Did you come here to worship or to flirt?"

The flirting was halted for a few peaceful moments with Ellie in Kyle's lap and Harmony snuggled up next to him. When everyone rose to sing a few songs before the sermon, Marjorie made Ellie sit between Harmony and Lucas, saying, "An old woman like me needs more room on this bench than you're giving me."

When they sat back down for the sermon, Kyle leaned back, fighting to keep the victory of having Harmony away from Lucas from showing on his face. Kyle rested his arm on the back of the bench, hardly registering what that would look like to people watching: a famous hockey player with his arm around his daughter's nanny. Yeah, that's exactly what he needed right now. But somehow, that prospect didn't bother him. Somehow, it just felt so right with Harmony tucked under his arm and Ellie laying her head on Harmony's lap. Just like it should always be that way. Forever.

*****

Harmony walked into the kitchen with some dirty dishes from the Sunday brunch everyone had just eaten. In reality, she was trying to avoid Lucas. He'd been acting so strange lately. He acted as though he might have feelings for her, yet whenever they spoke, he intimated that they were only friends. She supposed it didn't matter either way. She didn't love Lucas. *And you can't let yourself love Kyle.*

Harmony bit her lip and tried to focus. It was pretty hard seeing as the man in question was standing right in front of her. Kyle Taylor in the flesh. Harmony felt her heart flutter, and suddenly, she felt the dishes in her hands slipping towards the floor. Before she had time to blink, Kyle was there, taking the plates from her before they crash to the ground.

127

"Here, let me help you with those."

Harmony looked up and felt as though electric shocks were buzzing through her. She had the strangest urge to run her fingers through his thick brown hair along with the greatest longing to be wrapped up in his strong embrace. *Snap out of it!*

"Uh, thanks." Harmony felt like such a doofus. Since when did she get tongue-tied around Kyle?

Oh, Lord. Help me, please. I want to honor and glorify You, and I promise to trust You with my feelings for Kyle. Whatever Your plan is, I know You'll work it out for the good of both of us, Harmony prayed silently while watching Kyle put the dishes into the dishwasher. She leaned forward on the island in the center of the kitchen, resting on her forearms.

"So, Kyle," she began, trying not to focus on how great he looked with the sleeves of his dress shirt rolled up to his elbows or how the dark-green colour made his brown eyes pop, "what did you think about the sermon on Joseph?"

Pastor Schmidt's message on the Genesis passage was focused on forgiveness and trusting God. Kyle turned towards her and leaned his hip against the granite counter. He looked thoughtful but crossed his arms across his chest in what she knew was defensive posture. He sighed and shrugged his shoulders.

"I guess I've always struggled with the forgiveness thing. I was always angry. Mostly, I was angry at God."

Harmony frowned, tipping her head to one side. There was definitely more to Kyle than what meets the eye.

"Why would you be mad at God?" she ventured to ask. Harmony saw a flash of vulnerability fly across his features, so brief that she almost wondered if she had imagined it. Judging by the hard-set guarded expression he was sporting now, she hadn't. After a long moment of silence, Kyle spoke up.

"Why would my mom get cancer again? How can I not be angry?"

Harmony's heart went out to him and compassion overwhelmed her. *Oh, God. Please help him to understand.* Harmony walked around the island to where Kyle was standing and took both his hands in hers.

"Kyle," she said, looking him in the eye, "do you think it would be right to follow God because of what he can do for you or because you love him?" She sighed. "Let me put it this way: would you want to marry someone who married you because of what you can do for her or because she loves you?"

Kyle's gaze was intense as he whispered, "Because she loves me."

Harmony felt a blush creeping from her neck to her cheeks and she mentally kicked herself. *Way to go, Harmony,* she thought to herself. *That was probably the worst example possible, considering your present emotional state.* Why, oh, why did she use marriage as an example? Couldn't she have thought of anything a little less personal? She knew that she should distance herself from Kyle, but she couldn't force herself to move. The scary part was that she didn't even want to.

"That's how it is with God," she said, her whisper barely audible as she became aware of how close she and Kyle were standing. She rubbed her lips together, wondering what it would feel like to have Kyle kiss her. She tilted her face up as every last shred of reason left her and Kyle's arms encircled her waist. His lips were just inches from hers when—"Daddy?"

Harmony jumped back and was instantly filled with shame and remorse. She'd almost kissed him. How could she? She was just about to kiss her non-Christian boss. Wow.

"I'm just going to, um, well, uh, leave."

And not come back. Ever. Well, that was a little less likely, considering the fact that this was her job. Ugh. Harmony hoped Ellie hadn't seen anything.

"Daddy, you were gonna kiss her, wight? Wike de widdle mermaid or Cindewella?" Ellie's clear voice carried through the arched doorway of the kitchen as Harmony hurried upstairs to her room. So much for the idea of Ellie not seeing anything. Great. What type of nanny was she? Harmony practically bolted to her room and shut the door, leaning heavily against it and gasping for breath. She slid down and wrapped her arms around her knees, burying her head in the crook of her arms.

"Oh, God," she prayed as tears slipped out of her bright blue eyes. "Lord, why, oh, why would you let me have feelings for him? Why couldn't you have made him mean and cruel and ugly? Why does he have to be so considerate? Why does he have to look at me like he cares, laugh with me, or even listen to me? Lord, please help me!"

Harmony buried her head in her arms and cried. Why did she have to fall in love with someone that she could never ever be with? Someone who didn't share her faith, the most important part of her life? None of this would have happened if Roger hadn't died. If he had survived, they would be married by now, living in a remote part of Indonesia and working at their own mission. She never would have even met Kyle. She never would have met Ellie. Or Marjorie, or Lily, or... She sighed and wiped away her tears. Harmony knew she didn't regret meeting any of the people she had met in the past couple of months. Not even Kyle. Harmony sighed. Especially not Kyle.

If she lived to be a hundred, she would not forget the way Kyle made her feel. How he could make her feel wanted, cherished, and maybe even loved all at the same time. How he could make her laugh till she cried and how he made her look at life from a perspective she never would have considered. She realized that she would not trade the past few months for the world lest she miss seeing how Kyle and Ellie had bonded over the course of her stay at the Taylor House. Harmony grabbed her Bible from her bedside table and sat down in the plush window seat to have some heart-to-heart time with the One who created her. Lord knows she needed it.

*****

Harmony was a distraction. She always had been, but now it was certain. Kyle sighed and slammed angrily on the steering wheel. It wasn't that he didn't want to think about her; in reality, he'd rather *be* with her. The problem was he was thinking about her when he should be thinking about something else. He thought about her at practice, he thought about her at home. He thought about her when he was with Lily, Marjorie, and definitely when he was with Ellie. He thought about her when he should be thinking about his mom.

Marjorie had called just before he left practice to remind him that she needed to go for her ultrasound right away. She had already told Harmony, but they were still keeping Lily in the dark. Kyle pulled into the garage and exited his new luxury SUV.

Harmony had been avoiding him for the past few days after he had almost kissed her. He probably shouldn't have—no, he really shouldn't have, but she'd just looked so…perfect. And the way she talked about God almost had him believing her. Almost.

He plopped his hockey bag down by the laundry room then proceeded to the kitchen where, more often than not, the women of the house congregated. How was he supposed to bring his mom to the hospital to have her ultrasound without Lily knowing and getting herself all worked up?

Ellie was sitting, sprawled out in the hallway just outside the kitchen with her colouring books when he came in. When she heard him coming, she looked up and a smile broke out on her face, bright enough to light the whole house. Ellie threw aside her crayons and jumped into his arms.

"Daddy!"

She wrapped her little arms around his neck and buried her face in his shoulder. "I wove you, Daddy," she whispered in his ear.

Kyle felt like his heart was melting in his chest at the unreserved love given from his daughter, his baby. He looked down at her bright face rosy with health, her bouncing blond curls, and her sparkling brown eyes, finding himself thinking that if he and Harmony had kids, that's what they would look like. *Whoa, whoa, whoa. Wait, who said anything about kids? Or even about marriage?* Kyle had to stop letting his mind wander like that. He smiled down at Ellie and carried her into the kitchen, setting her down in her chair beside Harmony.

"Hey, Mom. You ready to leave?" Kyle wasn't exactly sure how this was much of a plan, but maybe if he made it seem like it was no big deal and they were just going out, nobody would be suspicious. Ellie's head popped up and she looked up at him with a frown furrowing her brows.

"But, but Daddy, you dust got home," she whined, coming over to him and wrapping her arms around his legs, her lower lip quivering and her eyes filling with tears. Nothing like his child to make him feel loved.

"Uh, don't cry, sweetie. I, uh, Grammy and I just have something we got to take care of, okay?"

"Can I come wit you? Pwease?"

Kyle was at a loss of what to say. He had no idea how long they would have to be at the hospital, and it would be much harder to keep their whereabouts a secret with Ellie around. He looked desperately at Harmony who seemed to be as unsure of what to do as he was.

"I, uh…"

Ellie stepped back and folded her hands, tucking them under her chin. She stuck out her lower lip and looked up at him imploringly.

"Pwwweeaase?" She said, stretching out the word persuasively. She had that puppy-dog look down to a science. He would have to be absolutely heartless to resist.

"Oh, all right," he said, smiling as she jumped up and squealed. Harmony looked up at him.

"Do you want me to come too?"

He shook his head, thinking it would be better with as few people as possible.

"You should take advantage of the rest of the day off."

Lily looked up from the magazine she was reading. "Oh, I'll join you instead."

Well that wasn't going to work. Not at all. Before Kyle could even open his mouth to protest Harmony spoke.

"Oh well, I thought that since I have the rest of the day off, maybe you could…well, never mind. Don't worry about it."

Lily looked at her curiously before asking, "No, what? Come on. Tell me."

"Oh, I just thought that, you know, you've said that you would teach me to skate, so I thought maybe…" Lily nodded her consent and turned back to Kyle.

"Sorry, bro. You'll have to go without me this time. I have more important things to do." She turned around and winked at Harmony, and Kyle had the strangest urge to do the same. Nah, he'd rather take her in his arms and kiss her. That probably wouldn't be very wise. Nice, but not wise. Kyle knelt down and told Ellie to gather up some coloring books and other things to amuse herself while Marjorie went upstairs to get her purse.

Kyle almost had the urge to pray that everything would turn out all right. He almost wanted to believe that God cared and that he wasn't about to let him go through this alone. Somehow he just couldn't risk it. He wasn't about to risk those he loved. Which made him wonder, was he ready to risk his heart?

When they got to the cancer clinic, Kyle told the receptionist that they'd arrived and took a seat beside Marjorie, glad to see that there was a kids' table with toys for Ellie to occupy herself with. Marjorie reached over and took his hand, turning to look at him.

"Kyle," she started, "we need to talk."

Kyle's heart sank to the pit of his stomach and he shook his head. "Mom, don't—"

"It's about you and Lucas."

Kyle paused, frowning in confusion. "Me and Lucas? What do mean?"

Marjorie sent him a pointed look. "I've seen what's been going on between you two, and I know exactly what it's about. It's about Harmony."

Kyle opened his mouth to argue, but he shut it when he realized that he couldn't honestly say it wasn't true. Things *had* been strained between himself and Lucas, and it *was* because of Harmony. Kyle couldn't deny that he had strong feelings for her, and knowing that Lucas did too had made things…difficult.

"He's your best friend," Marjorie continued. "And you need to remember that. Lucas has been by your side through thick and thin. Ever since you two played on the same team in minor league hockey, he's always had your back. He's part of the reason that you wanted to be traded here, part of the reason that you got…oh, what's her pickle, *that* woman to look into getting you traded here in the first place."

Kyle chuckled, rolling his eyes at his mother. "You mean Cassandra?"

"Oh yes, that's it. Anyway," she gave his hand a tight squeeze. "I just wanted to remind you that Lucas has been, and likely always will be, your best friend. I love Harmony and I think that you do too, but if you truly care about Lucas and Harmony the way I think you do, you'll want what's best for both of them."

At that moment, the ultrasound technician called Marjorie's name, and as she gave his hand a final pat, Marjorie added, "Besides, I don't think you have to worry about Lucas and Harmony becoming an item. Something tells me they don't feel that way for each other."

Kyle blew out a breath and rested his head on the wall behind him as he watched Marjorie walk away. She was right, of course, as she usually was. Lucas didn't deserve to be treated the way Kyle had been treating him lately, and even if he was interested in Harmony, he'd proved himself to be a great friend just for putting up with Kyle's miserable attitude of late. No matter what, Kyle *did* want what was best for both Lucas and Harmony. Oh, and one more thing.

He was in love with Harmony.

Chapter Twenty-Two

Harmony sat on the bench by the ice rink while Lily tied her skates. She had borrowed an extra pair of figure skates that Lily had lying around. They had to be tied a lot tighter than she had originally thought, and she wondered for the umpteenth time how she was going to manage this. She was clumsy enough on land, let alone on ice. She had to keep reminding herself that she was doing this for Marjorie.

Harmony sent up a quick prayer for Marjorie's well-being and tried not to let her apprehension show on her face. Lily didn't know what was going on and she wasn't about to hear it from her.

Harmony couldn't understand how Lily was so graceful even as she walked the short distance between the bench and the rink before stepping out easily onto the ice and turning around to face her. All she had to do was stand near Lily in order to feel like a toad beside a princess.

Harmony waddled over to the ice, took one step, and landed flat on her backside. Now she appreciated the fact that Lily had made her wear a helmet. Lily laughed and skated over to her, reminding Harmony of a quote she had once read: "A good friend helps you up when you fall down, a best friend laughs at you while you are on the ground." She was very glad she'd found a best friend in Lily.

Lily tried to teach her to simply skate forward, but unfortunately, Harmony's lack of grace and coordination prevented her from doing even the easiest things. At length she gave up and shuffled around on her hands and knees, much to Lily's amusement and annoyance. Lily glanced at her watch and frowned.

"Do you have any idea where they were going? They've been gone for over an hour." Harmony shook her head, trying to think of what to say without revealing the truth or telling a lie.

"I really can't say." Well, that was true. Thankfully, Lily took that for an answer, but she remained distracted until they saw the headlights coming up the driveway. Harmony's heart skipped a beat when Kyle got out and walked around to help his mother out of the car. She tried to no avail to convince herself that it was concern for Marjorie and not for any feelings she may or may not have towards Kyle. *And no more "almost" kisses, you hear that?* Harmony warned herself mentally and strengthened her resolve. Or at least she tried to. She knew that one look into those chocolate-brown eyes and she'd be a goner.

It had gotten much darker than Harmony realized, thanks to the floodlights surrounding the ice rink, and she could only see the silhouettes of the three people exiting the vehicle. The smallest one waved and said something, though Harmony could not hear exactly what was said. Lily was off the ice before Harmony even had a chance to stand up, and she yelled at her in surprised dismay.

"Lily, where are you going? You can't just leave me here."

Harmony began to feel a little bit frantic. The rink seemed so much larger when she was out in it all alone. Plus, she was curious to find out how the ultrasound had gone. Harmony hastened to stand up only to fall back onto the ice, where she lay sprawled out on her stomach for a minute.

"What on earth are you doing?" The deep voice startled her, and she turned to look even though she knew without a shadow of a doubt who it was. Kyle was leaning against the boards encircling the rink, the amused expression on his face making him look even more appealing. Harmony raised herself up on her forearms rather than trying to stand up, knowing that she would only end up falling and making a fool of herself. Okay, making more of a fool of herself.

"I'll have you know that I am learning to skate," she said with dignity. Kyle laughed.

"If you had said that you were trying to swim and couldn't figure out why it wasn't working, I might have believed you."

At her annoyed expression, he laughed again, brown eyes twinkling.

"By the way," Kyle lowered his voice to a mock whisper and leaned forward conspiratorially. "It's not real ice."

Harmony huffed, rolling her eyes. "No, really?"

Kyle laughed, the sound causing something warm and comforting to unfurl in her heart. "All right, but answer me this: how do you expect to learn to skate on your stomach?"

Harmony opened her mouth to reply, but seeing that she had nothing quick or witty to say, she only glared at him, making him laugh again and shake his head. Harmony was barely able to stop herself from smiling; she loved to hear him laugh, and if he thought her clumsiness was funny then so be it.

"Wait right there," Kyle called over his shoulder as he walked away.

"Like I have a choice," Harmony mumbled to herself while pushing herself into a seated position. She heard footsteps coming from the side of the rink and heard the crunch of hard snow between two boots.

"Kyle?" she called. "Kyle, is that you?"

"Mmmhmm."

"What are you doing?" Harmony thought he must be sitting on the bench, but from where she sat on the ice, she couldn't see or be certain.

"I'm coming to help you."

Harmony could see him and realized that he intended to join her on the ice. Her alone with Kyle on the ice in the dark with him helping her to skate? Hmm…not such a good idea. "No, no, wait. Stop." Harmony held out her hands as if she could mentally block him from coming out onto the ice. Kyle stopped, his skate inches from hitting the ice.

"What, you don't want help?" His brows knit together and he looked slightly insulted, but Harmony was not about to risk falling for him. Well, falling farther for him. Or was it falling harder for him?

"I... I'm fine. Thanks," she said quickly, surprised to see him back up and shrug his strong shoulders.

"All right, fine," Kyle paused a moment before adding: "Do you want me to bring you a blanket?"

"What?" Harmony looked up, completely confused.

Kyle shrugged again and tipped his head to one side. "I figured that if you were going to spend the night out here, you might want a blanket."

Harmony looked at him incredulously. "Why would I be spending the night out here?"

He leaned forward and leveled her with his gaze, eyebrows raised and the corner of his mouth raised in a half-smile.

"Well, you can't skate, so how are you supposed to get off the ice without any help?"

He just had to ask, didn't he? She supposed he had a point. She could always crawl off the ice, but that wouldn't be much fun.

"All right," Harmony sighed, steeling herself against his deep brown eyes and lethal charm. He skated over to her with the same grace as his sister, only it was a strong, masculine grace as opposed to his sister's runway-model grace. Once he reached her, he dropped down beside her.

"Here, let me show you how to get up."

The minute he had helped her to her feet, Harmony wobbled and fell directly into his arms. She gasped and pushed away, the momentum throwing her backwards and would've caused her to fall on her backside had not Kyle grabbed and steadied her. Thankfully, he held her away from him, keeping space between them and preventing any more embarrassing moments. Hopefully. Kyle held her hands and skated backwards in front of her, pulling her around the rink and instructing her on how to move her feet.

"It's basically like walking," he said as he stopped her from falling for what seemed like the umpteenth time.

"Well, we both know how great I am at that," Harmony returned dryly, causing a slow smile to spread across Kyle's face, one that warmed her heart and turned her insides to mush. She and Kyle actually got quite a bit accomplished. He taught her how to stop, and

though she couldn't skate on her own, she was at least able to somewhat keep her balance. At one point Kyle stopped, and she slammed
against his chest, looking up at him quizzically.

"Why don't you skate backwards now?"

Harmony almost laughed out loud at the thought. "What do
you mean? I can barely skate forward."

"Just try it, okay?"

Harmony hesitated for a moment, and Kyle smiled and
squeezed her hand reassuringly. Harmony sighed and consented, and
after watching Kyle, she attempted to skate backwards while he held
her hands. The outcome could not have been more disastrous. In
usual Harmony fashion, she tripped and managed to pull Kyle down
along with her. Harmony opened her eyes to see Kyle's handsome
face staring into hers and his brown eyes welling up with concern.
Harmony's cheeks heated and tingles went up and down her spine.
Her breathing grew thick and she had the strangest urge to run her
fingers through his hair. Harmony could feel the heat radiating from
his body. He was so close. Kissing close.

"Harmony? Are you okay?"

"I...you're kinda...squishing me."

Kyle hurried to his feet and pulled Harmony up with him.

"You're sure you're okay?"

Harmony could only nod, the words stuck in her throat, her
mind made fuzzy by the closeness of his presence, the whiff of his
cologne, the chocolate-brown colour of his eyes. Somehow, she
couldn't think, could barely breathe. The only thing that she saw
clearly was Kyle, and for one brief, crazy second, she imagined what
it would be like being married to Kyle, bearing his children and having so many more memories like this one. Kyle was leaning closer, his
hand cupping her jaw, his gaze dark and loving, and Harmony felt
her resolve wavering then slipping away completely, until all that she
cared about was here and now, and she closed her eyes and...

Bang!

Kyle's forehead connected with the visor of her helmet, and at
the same moment, Harmony heard the rumbling of an engine as
another car drove up into the driveway. Harmony was not particu-

larly surprised to see Cassandra exit the vehicle. Although Harmony was definitely not very pleased about it, the woman had not been to the house for three whole days, forever in whatever world Cassandra was living in.

For a minute, Harmony thought Kyle might kiss her anyway and she almost wished he would, but Cassandra sauntered over and called to Kyle, giving Harmony a chance to run, hide, anything to avoid the traitorous emotions that were conflicting within her being.

Forgetting everything Kyle had just taught her, she fell to her knees and scooted across the ice towards the exit. Stumbling into the house, she found Lily and Marjorie sitting and staring out the window, turning to look at her with embarrassed expressions mixed with a slight dose of indignation, like two children caught with their hands in a cookie jar—not sorry so much for what they did, but sorry that they were caught. Harmony fumbled with the laces on her skates before finally managing to kick them off.

"Ellie's up in her room," Lily said, smiling sheepishly at her.

"Thank you. I'll go tuck her in."

Harmony forced herself not to run up the stairs, scrounging up what was left of her dignity and calmly walking to Ellie's room. She paused at the top of the stairs, leaning against the wall and pressing a hand to her heart.

"God, I don't think I can do this," she whispered into the dim hallway. "God, this is too hard." Harmony felt like screaming. She had never meant for this to happen, never meant to fall in love with Kyle. For the first time, she understood the pain of loving someone that she could never be with.

Tucking Ellie in for the night only made the pain worse. As she kissed the little girl's forehead, she realized that Kyle wasn't the only one she had fallen completely and utterly in love with. Harmony loved Ellie with every fibre of her being, and she wished more than anything to be able to call the little girl her own.

Once in her room, Harmony fell to her knees before the Father, letting her tears fall for what could never be.

Kyle would much rather have followed Harmony inside than stand and listen to Cassandra's empty talk about nothing that was of any importance. He had wanted to kiss Harmony so badly that it almost hurt. If it hadn't been for that stupid helmet, he would have. Kyle's brows furrowed as he wondered about a niggling sense of doubt. He loved Harmony and he felt like she might love him too—no, he was certain of it—but he also felt like something was holding her back.

Kyle smiled slightly to himself. He loved her. He was in love with Harmony Clark, and though he didn't know what she was worried about, he wanted to scoop her up into his arms and kiss away her worries and her cares. Somehow, he didn't think that would be happening anytime soon.

"Kyle? Yoo-hoo." Cassandra's affected voice broke through his thoughts and made him entirely too angry. Kyle turned towards her and spoke through gritted teeth.

"What is it, Cassandra?"

Cassandra either didn't notice or didn't care. "What were you doing with that nanny when I drove up?"

"None of your business," Kyle barked back. Kyle hated the way she said "that nanny." He was also very tempted to say, "Trying to kiss her until you so rudely interrupted," just to see the look of shock or horror that would doubtless be displayed on Cassandra's face. Cassandra held her hands up in surrender, and then, looking at him with an over-the-top concerned glance, she said: "Just be careful, okay, Kyle?"

Kyle groaned inwardly, seriously doubting whether Cassandra really cared about his well-being.

"Is there a point to your visit? I have a lot on my plate right now, and I'm not going to stand here and waste my time if it's not worth my while."

Cassandra's face took on an almost evil look; her lip curled and she practically snarled as she said, "Oh yes, because Little Miss Nanny is sooo important."

Kyle turned around and glared at her, his expression catching her off guard. "You know what? Lay off Harmony; she's twice the woman you are." Kyle started to walk away, ready to leave the rude, opinionated woman standing in the snow when he turned around. "And if you are going to come around just to trash the people who live in my house, then maybe you shouldn't come at all."

Cassandra coughed and sputtered, hurrying to excuse herself.

"Oh, Kyle, you know I'm only joking, don't you? Besides, I'm certain Harmony is absolutely wonderful, if you like that boring, doormat type."

"She is nothing like that," Kyle snapped, his brown eyes turning nearly black with anger.

"Right. Of course, Kyle, I didn't mean it. I actually came to go over that new endorsement contract, it should only take a minute." Kyle was walking to the door before she even finished her sentence. "Fine" was all he said.

Chapter Twenty-Three

Kyle had said his goodbyes the night before, and he was up early to meet the team at the airport in preparation for two back-to-back away games. Kyle boarded the plane behind Scott Little, and he was not entirely unhappy to have a reason not to sit beside Lucas. Kyle liked Scott for his quiet and honest nature, and he appreciated the fact that if someone told Scott something confidential, no one would ever hear it from him. Right now, Kyle really needed someone to talk to; he was so confused, and nothing seemed to be working out the way it should. He just didn't know where or how to start.

"Hey, man," Kyle began rather uneasily, settling into his seat by the aisle. "How's it going?"

"Fine, and you?"

"Oh, fine, fine." Kyle muttered, not making eye contact. Scott looked at him for a minute, probably not believing a word he said.

"Really? You look kinda down. Anything I can do to help?"

Kyle sighed and shook his head, running a hand down his face. "I don't think so, not unless you can cure cancer."

Scott shook his head. "I can't, but I know Someone who can. Your mom got cancer again?"

For a minute Kyle looked at him, forgetting to speak, then realizing that when Scott said he knew someone who could cure cancer, he meant God. Did God even care?

"She might. We haven't got the results of her ultrasound back yet, so we can't be sure."

"That's unfortunate, man. I'll be praying for you."

Kyle looked at him, knowing that he didn't have to beat around the bush with Scott.

"Do you really think God even cares? That He even listens?"

Scott looked at him right in the eye, his gaze nonjudgemental but honest and his voice laden with conviction. "I believe he does. The Bible says that He is like a father to His children, a shepherd to His flock. What kind of father doesn't hear or listen to his children? We may not always get the answer we want, but it's not because God's holding out on us, but because it's not necessarily good for us."

Kyle shook his head, a pained expression crossing his features. "How would it benefit my mom if she got cancer again? How would it benefit any of us? She and Harmony are constantly talking about the love of God and how He has a plan for all of us, but I just don't get it. I'm a dad, and I would never do anything to hurt my daughter. Never."

Scott was silent for a minute, deep in thought before he finally spoke.

"Bad things happen because of sin, and since we live in a sinful world, bad things will happen to us. Being a Christian doesn't insulate us from the cost of sin, but it gives us hope that despite the hard times we go through and the situations we face, God will never leave us nor forsake us and we will never be left to our own devices."

Kyle remained silent as Scott added, "Besides, the rain falls on the good and the evil."

Kyle and Scott talked the length of the journey—about God, His love and compassionate mercy, His atonement for the sins of His creation, and of the gospel. Scott said something about trusting God and laying everything—time, money, possessions, and people—at the foot of the cross of Christ. Kyle found himself surprisingly convicted, asking himself over and over whether he wanted to believe in God because he wanted life to be easy, or because he really believed that He was the One and Only and the Creator of the universe who loved him and sent His only Son to die for him. It was like what Harmony had said: was he going to follow God because of what God could do for him or because He was real and he loved Him?

Two days later, as they were flying home after winning both games. Kyle made a point to sit next to Scott again.

"Scott, I wanted to talk to you about what you said the other day. I've been thinking about it and, I want to become a Christian.

I… I just don't know how." Kyle found it hard to get the words out. He hadn't been sure that he'd be able to say them, but he was glad he did. Scott smiled and patted him on the back.

"I'm glad. I've been praying for you for a while now."

Kyle was a little embarrassed but actually very pleased at the thought that someone other than his immediate family cared enough about his spiritual health and well-being to pray for him, before he had even expressed a desire to know Christ.

"As to how," Scott continued, "the Bible says that all you have to do to be saved is confess with your mouth that Jesus is Lord and believe in your heart that God raised him from the dead. You just accept the free gift that God has given you and trust Him with everything you have and you will be granted eternal life and eternal hope, knowing that no matter what happens, whether you live or die, you belong to Christ and nothing can pluck you from his hand."

Kyle mulled over it in his mind, knowing that he was ready to trust God with his life, his love, and everything else. Even his mother. He looked at Scott beseechingly. "Will you pray with me?"

And right there and then, on the flight home, Kyle gave his life to Christ.

Late that night, when Kyle got home, he crept silently up the stairs, kissed his sleeping daughter good night, and made his way to his room. Kyle opened his closet doors and grabbed the old, dusty cardboard box that he had put some things he hadn't wanted but couldn't make himself give away when he left at the age of sixteen to play minor league hockey.

In the very bottom of the box sat the simple black Bible that his mother had given to him before he'd left, untouched and still in its protective plastic covering. Kyle took it out and slid his hand over the soft, black leather, and opening it to the first book of the New Testament, he began to read.

*****

Harmony was sitting at the island in the kitchen, sipping on a cup of hot chocolate while watching Ellie colouring and visiting with

Marjorie and Lily. Harmony was certain that she had her emotions under control and that she would be ready when Kyle came into the kitchen that morning, though he would probably still be sleeping since the team got in late at night after their game down in the States. She was surprised to see him come into the kitchen with a big grin on his face, especially since he wasn't really a morning person. Kyle came into the room and scooped Ellie into his arms, tickling her tummy and causing the little girl to giggle.

"Who's Daddy's little girl?"

Harmony exchanged glances with Lily and Marjorie. From the shocked expressions on both women's faces, neither of them had ever seen Kyle like this before. Neither had she. Something was definitely different about him; she just wasn't sure what it was. Kyle put the giggling girl down and headed over to where Marjorie was standing. He greeted them all warmly and then turned to his mother.

"Mom, I don't know if I ever say this enough, but," he wrapped his arms around her and actually lifted her feet off the floor, "I love you so much."

Lily looked wide-eyed at Harmony and mouthed, "Has he lost it?"

Harmony shrugged her shoulders, wondering the same thing. When Lily turned around, Kyle was at her side. "You know, Lil, I just wanted to say that I am really glad you came to live here. I know you didn't want to come and it wasn't under the best of circumstances, but it's really great to have you here." When Kyle turned towards Harmony, she could see Lily turn around to mouth something Marjorie who was looking just as stunned as the rest of them.

"Harmony," Kyle looked at her for a minute before breaking eye contact. "Hiring you as Ellie's nanny has been one of the greatest things that has happened to this family. You're great with Ellie and you have been a real blessing."

Marjorie called to Kyle as he grabbed a protein shake packet and put it in the blender with some ice and some yogurt. "Kyle, do you have a drug problem? We can get you help, you know. Really, I heard about these interventions on TV."

Kyle just smiled and shook his head. Since when was he so good humored? Not that he was ever especially crabby, but he was never so...jolly? No, that wasn't it. Content. Harmony couldn't help but think of this Kyle as an improvement to the old Kyle. Who knew one road trip could change someone so much?

Kyle couldn't help but smile when he thought of the stunned faces of the three women in the kitchen. Only Ellie didn't seem fazed by his sudden transformation. Kyle nearly scared himself by the way one night had changed his life. He certainly couldn't blame anyone for their reactions. Kyle was making his way to the stairs when he heard the phone ring. Not even thinking about it, he picked it up.

"Hello?"

"Hello. This is the cancer clinic of Calgary. is Marjorie Taylor available?"

Kyle felt his stomach drop, making it nearly impossible to answer. *God, please don't let my mom have cancer.* Kyle stopped, considering what he'd just prayed. God wasn't a vending machine. *God, if she does have cancer,* Kyle prayed, *please give me the strength to bear it.*

Something he had read in Matthew the night before suddenly came to mind: "And behold, I am with you always, to the end of the age." Kyle felt his worry slip from his shoulders, and a peace he couldn't understand filled his soul.

It's okay, he felt the words whisper to his heart. *God's got a plan.*

Kyle walked back into the kitchen and gave the phone to his mother, amazed at how calmly he was able to do so. Marjorie took the phone casually and without a hint of trepidation. Kyle leaned his hip against one of the counters and watched his mother's face carefully. Her features twisted from ashen to dazed and ecstatic, then her eyes shone and a smile broke out on her face. Kyle knew exactly what the results from her test were just by looking at her expression, and he found himself grinning from ear to ear. He grabbed a pear from the fruit bowl on the counter and went downstairs to work out, with prayers of thanks seeping almost unconsciously from his soul.

Chapter Twenty-Four

Everyone had noticed that Kyle was different at practice today. Even his coach had commented on it. Only Scott knew what had happened on the flight home, and every time anyone mentioned Kyle's change in attitude, Scott just smiled. Kyle couldn't even explain the happiness he felt at having God change him so much.

He drove up the driveway humming one of the songs they had sang at church last Sunday. When he opened the car door, a bright pink bundle of energy screamed "Daddy!" before launching herself into his arms. Kyle was extremely glad to have the car to lean on, otherwise he probably would have toppled over. Another prayer of thanks flew from his heart. Only God could fix his relationship with his daughter, and God had sent Harmony to do it. Kyle was so thankful.

"Come pway wit us, Daddy."

Kyle felt glad that his daughter had asked him. It was snowing, but he had his heavy coat with him. Besides, he could use a little fun. And if Harmony was playing…

Wham!

An icy blast of snow hit him in the face, and Kyle found himself wiping away the remains of a snowball as Ellie and Harmony ran for cover.

It's on.

Kyle wished he'd thought to go inside and grab his gloves, but no way was he losing this battle. Behind his house were a couple acres of trees that Ellie always called "de woods." No doubt that was where she and Harmony were hiding. Kyle scooped up some snow and formed it into a ball, despite his frozen hands.

A snowball whizzed by and thudded against a nearby tree. Another one flew, this one only making it three or four feet out of a bunch of bushes. Kyle crept closer, hearing an eruption of giggles as two figures whizzed by, both going in either direction. All Kyle saw was a small flash of pink and a much taller flash of blue. He lunged for the blue one, snagging her around the waist as she yelled over her shoulder.

"Run, Ellie, run!" Harmony thrashed and twisted in her effort to get away, but it only ended in both of them falling into the snow. Kyle held her arms, pinning her down as she screamed and wiggled in an effort to push him off of her. They held eye contact for a split second and Kyle smiled. Harmony's eyes widened and she opened her mouth to scream before he shoved a handful of snow into her face.

Out of nowhere, Ellie came running and jumped on his back. Kyle turned over and rolled away from Harmony so that he could grab Ellie. Harmony threw a pile of snow in his face, laughing as he pretended to nearly drop Ellie. When the battle was finally over, they all lay laughing in the snow. Harmony punched him playfully. "You don't play by the rules."

Kyle raised his head to look at her. "There are rules?"

They all laughed at that one. Kyle's fingers were frozen solid and his jeans were soaked, but he couldn't remember ever having this much fun. Or ever feeling this tired. Ellie popped up with her usual endless supply of energy. How was *that* fair?

"I'm hungwy," she announced, getting up and pulling both him and Harmony to their feet. Kyle was never happier to smell the homemade pizza Clarissa was making. After changing into dry jeans and having a nice hot supper of barbeque chicken pizza and Caesar salad, he, Harmony, and Ellie went down to the theatre room to watch one of Ellie's favourite princess movies.

Sometime during the movie, Ellie, who was snuggled up in between the two of them, fell asleep. Kyle looked at Harmony and felt the ache of longing engulf him. What if...what if they got married? What if they spent the rest of their lives loving each other?

God, I don't want to mess this up. Please help me.

Kyle couldn't take his eyes off Harmony. She was breathtakingly beautiful, but what he admired most was her gentle, kind spirit. Harmony caught him staring and smiled. Then she frowned, looking down at Ellie, silently stroking her hair.

"Kyle," she whispered in the darkness of the theatre room. "What happened with Ellie's mother?"

Kyle felt his chest tighten and he looked away. Before he could start envisioning a future with Harmony, he knew that he needed to tell her the truth. He just hadn't expected it to hurt this much. Kyle sighed and ran his hand through his hair.

"I was at this party one night," Kyle didn't dare look at her, not wanting to imagine what she must think of him. "That's when I met Hilary. I liked her. She…she was fun to be with, always the life of the party."

Kyle looked down on Ellie, smoothing a hand over her silky blond hair. He wondered what it would feel like to run his fingers through Harmony's hair. *Not the time.* Kyle focused back on the tale of the agonizing truth about his past.

"When Mom got cancer, I didn't want to deal with it. I just wanted to forget. When I was with Hilary, I did forget. I forgot everything important. I didn't see her for another seven months until one day while I was waiting for Mom in the hospital."

Kyle swallowed hard, the shame of what he'd done magnified by his new Christian faith. *God, forgive me.* "She was pregnant and she claimed that the baby was mine. And it was."

Kyle swallowed hard, gritting his teeth together and tamping down the surge of anger he felt when he thought of Hilary. "She knew that Mom was having cancer treatments, and she came to the hospital every day until I ran into her. She had me pay her not to have the late abortion she was planning on. She left the day after Ellie was born."

Kyle felt his heart sinking. Harmony could never love someone with his past, someone like him.

Harmony sat stunned into silence as she listened to Kyle's gut-wrenching tale. Kyle refused to look at her during his story, and

even now, he avoided her gaze. Harmony couldn't believe that someone would do that. That a mother would be so callous as to make the
father of her child pay not to have her abort his baby. That anyone
would use an infant as a means of making money. Harmony looked
down at the sleeping girl snuggled up in between them and thanked
God for His mercy in saving this child.

"I'm glad," she stated quietly, turning towards Kyle. "I'm glad
you didn't let her abort Ellie."

Kyle looked at her for a minute then nodded, looking down on
Ellie and stroking her hair. "Me too." There was a moment of silence
when Kyle asked a question in turn.

"What happened to your fiancé?"

Harmony paused, waiting for the familiar pain in her gut that
always accompanied thoughts of Roger's death. Strangely, now that
she had come to terms with the fact that she was not responsible for
what happened to him, it hurt less to talk about how he died.

"We were putting on a church service and potluck lunch for the
people in the village where we worked," Harmony explained. "There
was a flash flood and a little girl was out in the middle of the torrent,
hanging onto a big rock." Harmony took another deep breath, blinking away the sting of tears. Just because Roger's death hurt less didn't
mean it didn't hurt at all. "Roger dived in and saved her." Harmony
swallowed hard before continuing, "he died of a lung infection three
days later." A single tear slipped down Harmony's cheek. "By the
time he died, he was so delirious he didn't even know who I was."

"Oh, Harmony," Kyle said softly, placing a comforting hand on
her shoulder.

"All this time," Harmony said, "I thought it was my fault. I was
in charge of taking care of the kids. If I had been doing my job, that
little girl wouldn't have been out there in the first place and Roger
never would have died."

"Harmony, it wasn't your fault. Some things are just out of our
control."

Harmony smiled at him, her eyes still shining with tears. "I
know that now."

There was another moment of silence when Ellie stirred. Harmony glanced at her watch. No wonder Ellie had fallen asleep; it was hours past her bedtime. "I should probably put this little one to bed," Harmony stood, picking Ellie up and cradling her in her arms.

"Wait," Kyle called to her, standing up and holding out his arms. "Can I carry her?" Harmony nodded, handing him the sleeping angel. A lump rose in her throat as she watched him, cradling the little girl against him. Oh, how she loved them.

She must love him a whole lot if she had told him the one thing that no one really knew: her feelings of responsibility over her fiancé's passing. She held a hand to her forehead, feeling suddenly very dizzy. So she loved Kyle. The question now was what was she going to do about it?

*****

Kyle couldn't stop thinking about Harmony's reaction to his revelation or about how she had trusted him with a revelation of her own. Then again, he couldn't stop thinking about her in general. But what was new about that? He thought about her when he woke up, when he went down to the kitchen to grab his shake in the morning, when he tucked Ellie in at night, when he spoke to his mother, when he teased and tormented Lily, when he was at hockey practice or a game, and when he went to sleep at night.

Finally, he got up his gumption and asked his sister to come help him with some "errands." As they were driving down to the mall, he nearly regretted it.

"Why do you need me to come with you? Why are you even going to the mall? I didn't know you even knew where to find it." After a moment of silence, Lily persisted, turning in her seat to look at him. "So, are you going to tell me what this is all about?"

Kyle sighed. What happened to all that gumption he had a minute ago? "I, uh, sorta need, I guess you could say some female expertise on a…an engagement ring."

Lily squealed so loudly he nearly lost control of the vehicle. "That is so amazing! Thank goodness you are finally going to ask her. I mean, really, she moved in in August. You've had plenty of time."

All he could do was look at his excited sister incredulously out of the corner of his eye. Was she crazy? Three months was nothing! Even though he and Harmony had been living under the same roof all that time, they'd never even gone on a date. Maybe he was crazy.

Crazy or not, aside from the short time they had known each other, there wasn't anything really preventing him from asking Harmony to marry him. He knew without a shadow of a doubt that he loved her, that he would always love her, and by the grace of God, he would marry her and love her every day for the rest of his life.

Kyle shook his head in disbelief as he pulled into the mall parking lot. *Here goes nothing.*

Lily opened the passenger side door and nearly sprinted to the mall doors, no doubt instantly making her way towards her favourite jewelry shop situated inside. He found her inside and already looking intently at engagement rings.

"That one's pretty."

Kyle looked over his sister's shoulder and shook his head. It was nice, but it wasn't Harmony. He needed something that would suit her perfectly and would just scream *Harmony!* Kyle scanned every ring in the glass casings, feeling more and more disappointed by the minute knowing that nothing he'd seen would suit Harmony.

"I found it! Oh, I found it! Kyle, quick, come see!" Lily was nearly jumping up and down with excitement, reminding him of Ellie when she got wound up. Kyle looked over at the ring she pointed at and found himself grinning. It was perfect. The sales lady took out the ring and Lily tried it on her index finger and showed it to him.

"That should be perfect. Her hands are a little bit bigger than mine."

The sales lady named the price and Kyle paid with his credit card, signing the receipt. The sales lady looked at the receipt, then back at him, her eyes wide in surprise.

"Are you actually Kyle Taylor? As in *the* Kyle Taylor who plays centre for our NHL hockey team?"

Looking at the ring in the soft velvet blue ring box that was only a few shades darker than Harmony's eyes, Kyle resisted the urge to roll his eyes. In reality, the sales lady's curiosity didn't bother him.

He didn't think anything could. Kyle frowned as a niggling sense of doubt rose inside him. What if Harmony said no? What if she didn't, couldn't love him? He would just have to take that chance. The female clerk slid a piece of paper across the counter towards him.

"Do you mind signing this one too, just for a keepsake?" she asked shyly.

Smiling, Kyle signed the paper and he and Lily exited the mall and made their way through the parking lot.

Lily went on and on about how excited she was, how she was finally going to have a sister, and how happy she was that he finally came to his senses and bought Harmony a ring.

"Speaking of which," Lily said, pulling her door closed as she settled into her seat, "when are you going to pop the question?"

Kyle gulped and felt his hands go clammy. That was the million-dollar question. When would he ask her?

"I... I'm not sure."

Lily listed off several ideas and where the most romantic places to take a girl were, but Kyle only half-listened to her. This was by far one of the most important decisions of his life. What was more, could he put his heart on the line? Was he willing to do that? Why were all these doubts popping up now? Taking a deep breath, Kyle took his worries to the God who cared.

All right, Lord. I lay this at Your feet. Help me to do this right, and not to worry about what I can't control. I'm putting my trust in You.

Nevertheless, Kyle mulled over what to do and what to say all week. He found himself putting it off thinking: *Not yet, this isn't the right time. I'll just wait a little longer.* And a little longer... And a little longer...

Chapter Twenty-Five

Harmony couldn't take it. Not anymore. She had to fall out of love with Kyle, and she needed to do it now. She just wasn't quite sure how. She didn't want to quit her job, she didn't want to leave Ellie, Lily, Marjorie…or Kyle. She really didn't want to leave Kyle. Harmony sighed. *Lord, why does this have to be so hard? Why did I have to fall in love with Kyle?*

Harmony looked around at the mess she and Ellie had created. Ellie was determined to make the perfect "I love you" card for her daddy. Around them lay sheets and sheets of coloured paper, cut-out flowers, hearts, and hockey sticks. Some of them looked really cute, yet when each one was finished and laid out in front of the little girl, they were all pronounced inadequate. Ellie sighed angrily, tossing a marker and some glitter pens to the side.

"Dey not good 'nough, notting good 'nough."

Harmony smoothed a lock of Ellie's hair off her forehead.

"I'm sorry, sweetheart. It's going to have to wait till tomorrow; it's just about bedtime."

Ellie sighed mournfully.

"Alwight."

Harmony tried to banish thoughts of her true feelings for Kyle from her mind and was happy to tuck Ellie in that night, knowing that she would be searching the Scriptures for answers long into the night.

Kyle woke up that night, the pain in his abdomen taking his breath away. He tried to lay still for a minute, hoping that the pain would lessen if he just stayed quiet. Instead, it got worse. A few minutes later, Kyle rushed to the washroom and promptly threw up. Kyle splashed cold water on his face, trying to fight the waves of nausea that hit him like a hurricane. He couldn't get sick. He had a super important game against one of the biggest rival teams scheduled for the next day. The team needed him. "Oh, God, please make it stop," Kyle moaned, grabbing a couple of ibuprofen before going back to bed and lying awake well into the early hours of the morning.

*****

Harmony had finally found the perfect solution to Ellie's card problems. She had printed what felt like a million pictures of Kyle in his hockey gear off the Internet. Ellie had used pink paper to cut out a giant heart and was cutting out all the "daddy pictures" to glue to it, with a nice big one of Kyle pasted right in the middle of it.

Harmony was having a lot of fun helping the little girl cut out the pictures, but she found herself thinking more and more about Kyle. Where was he? How was he doing? He had an important game tonight. Was he nervous? He hadn't eaten anything all morning; he didn't even come in to get his protein shake. Should she be worried? Why couldn't she get him out of her head?

Ellie's sweet voice pulled Harmony out of her reverie.

"I need mow pictures, pwease," she said, looking up at Harmony with her doe-brown eyes. "I need mow daddy pictures."

Harmony cocked her head to one side, looking at the pile of untouched pictures sitting beside the little girl.

"What's wrong with these ones?"

"No," Ellie said decisively. "Not dos ones."

"I don't have any more pictures," Harmony explained, holding up her hands in the I-don't-know fashion that adults often use with children.

Ellie stood up angrily with contorted features, and she looked ready to cry. "But I *need* mow pictures!"

Harmony took a deep breath, bracing her for the tantrum that was about to ensue. At that moment, a shadow crossed the doorway. Harmony turned around to see Cassandra peeking around into the room, a look of innocence etched on her features. Harmony's suspicions rose almost immediately, though she felt a bit bad for thinking the worst of Cassandra. She was determined to look for the good—if there was any—in the arrogant, selfish, rude woman standing in front of her. Harmony nearly grinned at the irony. She wasn't off to a very good start. Cassandra spoke up.

"I heard what you two were talking about, and I think I may be able to help."

Cassandra made sure to keep the innocent expression pasted on her face as she smiled what she hoped was a kind, trustworthy smile. She had just come back from putting the vintage set of hockey cards Kyle had been trying to buy for nearly two years on his desk. They had cost thousands of dollars and they were ridiculously rare; she was certain that if anything were to happen to them, that would be the last straw. She almost giggled with glee as she told Harmony about the old hockey cards that Kyle was planning to throw away. The little girl—what was her name again?—was getting more excited by the minute. Cassandra was certain that her plan would work perfectly, seeing as how much power the little girl had over her bewitched nanny.

"Well…" Harmony turned to look at her with those clear, pristine blue eyes and lovely features that always made Cassandra want to be sick. "I'm really not supposed to go into Kyle's office at all…"

Cassandra dismissed that idea with a wave of her had.

"I don't see why it would be such a big deal. Kyle won't even miss those old cards." Cassandra looked at Harmony and the little girl pleading by her side, and she knew she had won. Before she knew it, Harmony would be out of her life for good. And there would be nothing standing between her and Kyle. Finally, her life was coming back into its proper order. And that order did not include Harmony.

"I'd get them for you myself, but I really need to run," Cassandra said turning her nose up at the annoying nanny. "Anyway, I hope you come up with another plan so that the little darling can make her card."

Harmony had looked somewhat unsure until that moment. "Well, all right."

Cassandra turned to leave when Harmony called to her. "Aren't those the cards that Kyle has been trying to buy for so long? I don't want to take the wrong ones."

Cassandra grinned maliciously. Anyone as naive as Harmony deserved whatever they got. "Don't be ridiculous. Kyle would have those stored in a safe place."

Well, Cassandra smirked, *he would if he'd had the chance.* Cassandra turned on her heel, grabbed her purse and jacket, and left. The brisk cold and dreary weather did nothing to dampen her spirits.

Harmony had decided to trust Cassandra and take the cards for Ellie. In truth, she couldn't say that she wasn't surprised that Cassandra had even thought to help her with Ellie's project. Why, she didn't think that Cassandra even knew Ellie's name! Harmony shook her head. It didn't matter; her little angel was happy. Harmony felt such love for the little girl that she almost wished... *No!* Harmony spoke to herself firmly. *Don't think like that. You can't.* Tears stung the backs of her eyes and threatened to overflow from her closed eyelids. Harmony took a deep, steadying breath. She would not jeopardize her walk with God by becoming yoked together with a non-Christian. She had seen firsthand the trials that Christians who chose to marry non-Christians went through. That wasn't the life she wanted for herself or her future children.

"Miss Hawmony, wook. It's awe done." Ellie grinned at her, her earlier crisis having been averted.

Harmony looked at the big collage and smiled. The picture of Kyle was accented by pink glitter and heart stickers. All over the big heart card were pictures of Kyle, along with the faces cut out from the old hockey cards Kyle was getting rid of.

"It's beautiful, honey. Your daddy will love it."

"Wiw you hewp me write on it?"

Harmony smiled and gave Ellie a quick hug.

"Of course I will, sweetheart."

After Harmony had coached her through writing "I love Daddy" across the top, Harmony heard the door open. "That's your dad. Why don't you go give it to him? I'll just be in here, okay?"

"Okay" was Ellie's reply as she skipped away.

Kyle came home after sitting in the walk-in clinic for most of the day and having to leave before even being seen by a doctor so as not to be late for pregame warm-up. He felt worse than he had all day only to be greeted by the one thing he'd never been expecting. Ellie had come running into the foyer, holding up a big heart-shaped card with the words "I love Daddy" across the top. She had glued pictures on the card—most were of himself—but some were of other hockey players. And he had a sinking feeling that he knew exactly where she got them.

"It's beautiful, sweetheart. Where…where did you get the pictures?"

"Fwom Miss Hawmony." Ellie looked from him to the card and back again, her chin starting to wobble. "You don't wike it?"

"Oh no. I love it, sweetheart," he said half-heartedly. "Why don't you go upstairs and put that in my room where I can always see it?"

Kyle waited until Ellie was safely out of earshot before unleashing the extent of his anger. "Harmony!" Kyle stormed into the kitchen, nearly barreling into Harmony as he entered. She staggered back, a look of alarm on her face.

"Is everything all right, Kyle?"

"How could you?" Kyle asked, leaning against the kitchen island, nearly doubling over, partly from the pain in his gut and partly at his anger towards Harmony. "How could you take my stuff and let Ellie chop it up for some silly card?"

Harmony stepped back, anger changing her features.

"Silly card? Do you know how long that child worked on that "silly card"? How many other times she started one card and then threw it away because it wasn't good enough for her daddy? How could you say something so thoughtless?"

Kyle nearly sputtered with fury. "Me, thoughtless? You're the thoughtless one. Do you know how long I've been trying to get those cards?"

Doubt flickered across Harmony's face, but instead of cooling his anger, it made it worse.

"But Cassandra said—"

"This isn't about Cassandra!"

Kyle wanted to punch something. All this time, he'd trusted Harmony. He thought that he loved her. Kyle clenched his jaw. He couldn't have been more wrong. He clutched the edge of the island, fighting another wave of nausea.

"I trusted you, Harmony. I trusted you with something important to me and you go—" This time, Harmony interrupted him.

"Something important to you? You trust me with your daughter every single day, and now you are referring to cards as something important to you?" Harmony shook her head in disgust. "I can't do this. Not anymore." She looked him in the eye, her expression defiant. Kyle balked. Why would she be acting like she was the one who was hard done by, the one who'd been wronged? She was the problem here! "Consider this my two weeks' notice."

Kyle shook his head. If she wanted to quit, that was just fine. He could find many more suitable, more experienced, and more responsible nannies who would, in the long run, be so much better than Harmony ever was.

"Don't bother with your two weeks' notice. Don't be here when I get back tonight."

With that, Kyle barreled out of the room in a rage, nearly knocking his startled mother off her feet in the process. He couldn't believe Harmony. Who would have thought that she would have the audacity to talk to him like that? And how could she do something so irresponsible like that, especially after having trashed his office? Kyle heard a car horn honk and he swept through the foyer, grabbing his hockey bag on his way out and slamming the door behind him.

Chapter Twenty-Six

Harmony sank down into the nearest chair, bursting into tears. Why did she say that? Why did she say she would hand in her notice? That was what lead to her getting fired. Fired! She loved this job! She loved Ellie! Why did Kyle have to freak out over some hockey cards?

Harmony's sobs of sadness turned to tears of rage. Cassandra set her up. She *said* that the cards were garbage, that Kyle wouldn't care, and he wouldn't even notice that they were gone. What did she do that made the woman hate her so much? Why would someone be so cruel? A noise from the doorway caused Harmony to raise her face. Marjorie stood in the archway with an alarmed expression on her face. Harmony wiped her eyes, trying to hide the fact that she'd been crying.

"Harmony, are you all right?"

"Yes, yes, fine." She drew in a steadying breath. Harmony hated lying, but she didn't want to worry Marjorie. Marjorie nodded.

"So the red blotches on your face and the tear streaks down your cheeks are just some wacked out fashion statement?"

Harmony sniffed, wiping her eyes again.

"Come on, honey. Nothing can be that bad. We can work it out."

Harmony felt the tears welling up in her eyes again. She shook her head. "I don't think so. I really blew it this time."

Marjorie wrapped a comforting arm around Harmony's shoulders.

"Why don't you just tell me what happened?"

"Cassandra set me up!" Harmony wailed, sobbing nearly uncontrollably. It was like the floodgates had finally opened and there was no stopping them. "Ellie cut up the cards… Kyle…we got in a fight...gave him my notice...told me not to be here to-tonight!" Harmony couldn't control her tears. She felt sick, angry, and stupid. She was really sick of Cassandra who, from day one had always been out to get her. She was angry at Kyle for reacting the way he did. And she felt stupid not only for trusting Cassandra, but also for losing her heart to the one man who could never have it.

"Oh, honey," Marjorie cooed, though from her tone of voice, Harmony knew that she'd only gotten about half of that. "I'm sure he didn't mean that. Maybe—"

Harmony stood up, shaking her head sadly. Kyle meant what he said.

"I...I'm leaving, Marjorie." Harmony took a steadying breath before continuing. "I should go get packed." Harmony nearly sprinted up the stairs to her room before Marjorie saw the sorrow in her face.

Kyle slammed the door as he jumped into the back of Scott's truck. Lucas was sitting in the front passenger seat, and he turned around to look at him quizzically as Scott pulled out of the driveway.

"Are you okay?"

"Am I okay?" Kyle didn't even try to keep the frustration out of his voice. "I just fired my nanny."

Lucas looked at him. "You did what?"

Scott glanced at him through the rearview mirror. "When you said you were going to propose, I didn't think that was how you planned it."

Kyle froze. Propose. Right.

"Nope. Not anymore."

Lucas had his mouth hanging wide open, his expression flabbergasted. "You meet a woman like that and you let her slip through your fingers? You fire her? What kind of insane idiot does that?"

"You don't know what she did," Kyle said savagely.

Lucas rolled his eyes mockingly. "What, she put too much ice in your protein shake? Or maybe Ellie is actually happy and that bothers you?"

Kyle glared at him.

Scott spoke up. "Seriously, Kyle, what did she do that was so bad that you can't forgive her?"

Kyle took a deep breath, trying to quell the ache in his stomach and fight the wave of nausea that nearly made him double over. "She took those hockey cards, the ones I spent two years trying to get, and let Ellie chop it up for some silly card that she gave me."

Scott slammed on the brakes, sending Kyle lurching forward. Thankfully, they had not yet reached the main road and there was not another car in sight.

"You fired her over hockey cards?"

Kyle comforted himself with a glare in Scott's direction, seeing that when he said it out loud, it sounded shallow. Really shallow.

"You aren't going to propose because of hockey cards?" Scott shot him an incredulous look before glancing at Lucas for support.

Lucas shook his head. "Do you mean to say that you are going to be miserable for the rest of your life because your daughter made you a card for no reason other than the fact that she loves you? Is that what you're telling us? 'Cause if it is, I think we've got a problem."

"If you like Harmony so much why don't you propose?" Kyle spat out, not quite as angrily as before, as he was already dreading the ramifications of his impulsive decision.

"Is that what this is about?" Lucas glared at him dubiously. "You've got to be kidding me."

When Kyle didn't answer, Lucas turned to him irately. "You want to know the truth, blockhead? The truth is, I flirted with Harmony because you're a competitive idiot, and it was the only way to get you to man up and admit that you cared about her. You don't appreciate anything until you think that you might lose it. Well, here's a news flash: you are about to let the only woman you've ever loved walk out of your life because of some stupid hockey cards."

Scott was turned around in his seat and looked at him. "You know, Kyle, if we don't forgive others, God won't forgive us. Don't make a decision that you'll regret."

Lucas nodded vigorously. "Yeah, like a mistake that you will regret for your whole. Entire. Life."

Scott looked at Lucas and nodded. "Okay, now we're good."

Scott turned around and put the truck back in motion. Lucas stared straight ahead of him. Kyle leaned his head against the window, partly because he felt defeated and partly because he felt so hot. He shivered yet he felt like he was sitting in furnace.

"I'm going to be sick," he mumbled under his breath. Being angry actually lessened the pain in his abdomen, but now it came back at full force. Even worse than that, he was disgusted with himself. Scott and Lucas were right. It was just a bunch of hockey cards. And Ellie's card was really cute. Kyle groaned as he thought about how he had yelled at Harmony and told her to be gone before he got home.

Reality dawned on him nearly as painful as the stabbing sensation in his gut. He couldn't let her leave. He couldn't lose her. Kyle reached into his jacket pocket and felt the velvet box that contained the ring he wanted to give to Harmony. He needed her. Ellie needed her. His whole family needed her. And he loved her. He loved everything about her—her ready smile, her compassion for everyone that she met, and her protectiveness of Ellie. If he lost her, he didn't think that he would ever win her back. He needed to call home. Now.

Kyle reached into his other pocket and felt his heart drop. He'd forgotten his cell phone. Kyle could have banged his head through the window. Of all the days to forget his phone, it had to be today. Maybe he could borrow Lucas's.

Kyle moaned, the pain in his abdomen taking his breath away and pushing out all other thoughts. Yet it was only a dull ache compared to the pain in his heart. Lucas turned around, concern evident in his expression.

"You okay? You don't look so good. Maybe you shouldn't play tonight."

Kyle shook his head. "This is important, I have to play."

In reality, Kyle knew that if he didn't have something to do, he'd go crazy. If there had been time, he probably would have asked Scott to turn around and go back to his house so that he could apologize to Harmony, propose, and then kiss her senseless. Hopefully, he'd still have a chance. They pulled into the parking lot designated for players and then rushed into the changeroom. Kyle quickly changed into his hockey gear, fighting wave after wave of nausea that assaulted him. Finally, he rushed to the washroom and was sick again. Kyle leaned against the sink, trying to take it all in. What was wrong with him? Why was he so sick? And why was he becoming the biggest jerk on the planet?

"God," he moaned, "this isn't working for me. Please help."

Kyle joined the rest of the team, getting ready to get on the ice. Standing there on the ice and listening to the national anthem, Kyle felt like the world was spinning. His stomach hurt so bad and his breath was coming out in sharp ragged breaths. Even standing out there on the ice felt like he was in the middle of a furnace. What was happening to him? Scott looked over at him.

"Are you sure you're okay?" He whispered quietly.

Kyle nodded and steeled his resolve. Scott tapped the front of Kyle's shin with his hockey stick, a gesture of support. Kyle just tried to focus on the importance of this game. It didn't matter how bad he felt; he had to play. It was an important game, and no way was he going to leave his team without their top centre. He was still battling waves of nausea when the game started. He lost the faceoff, and then followed the opposing team sluggishly back towards his team's end of the ice. It was bad enough that it hurt to skate but getting hit so often really wasn't helping his cause.

Wait, he *never* got hit. Or at least, he rarely got hit. He was fast, had good reflexes, and was ultimately pretty untouchable. Kyle shook his head. What was wrong with him? Yet despite the fact that he was playing horribly, that his coach was madder than a wet hen, that he felt sicker than he'd ever been in his life, or that his team was losing, all he could think about was Harmony. He barely heard the earful his coach gave him when he got back to the bench. The only thing that mattered to him was Harmony.

Would she be there when he got back? Kyle felt his throat tighten. Why had he gotten so angry over a bunch of hockey cards? Was he really willing to lose her over worthless *things*? Kyle already knew the answer to that. No, he wasn't. He just hoped he'd have the chance to tell her. *God please help me make things right.* Kyle could only pray that she'd forgive him.

When the line changed, Kyle stepped back onto the ice. He was determined to do his best and fight through the pain. And pray that Harmony would be there when he got back. Lucas passed him the puck. Kyle skated up the ice, managed to swerve around two opposing players, and passed to another player on his team, despite the crippling pain in his stomach. A player from the rival team checked him up against the boards and Kyle fell like a ton of bricks.

The play didn't stop right away. It wasn't a bad, mean, or dangerous hit, but Kyle couldn't make himself stand up. He was in so much pain he had to coach himself through breathing. Just breathe. The ache in his abdomen was crippling. *God, what is going on?* Why was this happening to him? Why now? Now when everything else in his life was falling apart, this had to happen too.

Kyle heard the referee whistle the play dead. The next thing he knew, the paramedics were putting him on a stretcher and pushing him off the ice. Kyle remembered the paramedic asking him what was wrong; he'd only managed to moan out an answer about the pain in his stomach. He felt pretty out of it for a while, unable to focus on the conversations going on around him because of the gnawing fear looming like a dark cloud over him. Was he going to die like this? He wasn't really afraid to die; he knew that having accepted Christ, he didn't have to worry about ever seeing the ugly face of death.

What really troubled him was what would happen to his family. What would happen to Ellie? He could console himself with the fact that though she would doubtless miss him at first, she would move on and by the time she was older, he would only be a faint memory. But what about his mother and Lily? They would have to raise his daughter and always wonder whether or not he had ever actually accepted Christ. And then there was Harmony. Pain squeezed his heart, making him forget the pain in his stomach completely. If he died now, he'd never get to tell her how he felt about her, never get to ask her to marry him… *No.* Determination rose inside Kyle. He wasn't giving up. He wasn't going to surrender. Harmony would have to know how he felt about her. She had to. *God, please let me live to tell her.*

Chapter Twenty-Seven

Harmony fought back tears as she turned away from Ellie, putting another set of clothes into her suitcase.

"B...but Miss Hawmony, you can't weave! I need you! I... I wove you!" Harmony couldn't stand to hear her little girl crying. *Her* little Ellie. She turned around, opening her arms.

"Come here."

Ellie launched herself into Harmony's arms, clinging to her and sobbing her heart out while Harmony sat on the edge of the bed, rocking her gently and trying to comfort the little girl while inside she wanted to break down and bawl right along with her.

"I'm going to miss you so much," Harmony whispered hoarsely, squeezing her eyes shut.

"B-but w-why would you want to...to weave me?" Ellie hiccupped miserably.

"Oh, I don't, sweetheart," Harmony cooed, smoothing back the girls silky curls. "But you don't need me anymore. You have your daddy, Grammy, and Aunt Lily..."

"But I want you too!" Ellie wailed. Harmony leaned back so she could look Ellie in the eye.

"You have to be brave for me, sweetheart," she commanded gently, her own heart shattering into little pieces even as she said the words.

"You have to be good and strong, and always, always trust God. Will you promise me that?"

Ellie sniffed and wiped her nose with the back of her hand, nodding solemnly.

"I...I pwomise."

Harmony hugged her close. Ellie wrapped her little arms around Harmony's neck, resting her head in the crook of Harmony's neck and shoulder.

"If you were my mo…mommy, you wouldn't have to weave."

Harmony felt what was left of her heart break. The thought of being Ellie's mother and being Kyle's wife was a dream that would not—could not—ever become a reality.

"Come now," Harmony said, standing up and setting Ellie down on her feet. "Be strong for me, baby. Here, why don't you help me pack?"

Ellie helped her take her things out of the closet and drawers, always staying glued to Harmony's side. Harmony would do anything to take away the haunted, solemn look that was etched on Ellie's features. They continued like this in silence, just being in one another's company when Marjorie burst into the room. She looked pensive and scared, and Harmony had only seen her look like that when they thought that Kyle had been in the car accident.

"Harmony, I need to talk to you."

Alarmed at Marjorie's expression, Harmony left Ellie in her room and met Marjorie out in the hall.

"Lily just called. Kyle got hit during the game. It's bad, and we're going to meet her at the hospital." Marjorie wrung her hands agitatedly. "I'm really worried, Harmony."

Harmony's heart plummeted, and she squeezed Marjorie's arm encouragingly, as much for Marjorie as for herself. She tried desperately to keep her panic from showing on her face as she grabbed her jacket and purse and calmly explained to Ellie that her daddy was in the hospital and they were going to go there to see him. Ellie looked more afraid and anxious than she had since the day Harmony arrived, and her eyes were red and swollen from crying.

"Can I bwing Mookie?"

Harmony knew the little girl was vulnerable and afraid and needed all the love and comfort Harmony could give her. Harmony held up Ellie's big pink stuffed bunny. "Why don't you bring Mr. Bunnykins instead?"

Ellie took the toy solemnly, holding it against her chest. "He's not as good as Mookie."

"I know, sweetheart."

Everyone was silent on the drive to the hospital, and for the first time, Harmony was given the chance to let the gravity of their situation sink in. Kyle was hurt. Badly if they had rushed him to the hospital. She felt as though a rock had settled in her stomach, making it hard for her to breathe normally.

She couldn't lose him. She wouldn't survive. She loved him. Even though he didn't love her. Harmony felt tears welling up in her eyes. She loved him, but she couldn't do anything about it. She would still lose her job and still have to leave. All she could do was pray daily for his salvation and hope to one day see him in the realm eternal.

Harmony glanced in the rearview mirror to look at Ellie. Marjorie had been too shaky to drive, and Harmony thanked the Lord above that she'd still been home when they'd heard the news. Ellie's face was drawn and her eyes glazed as she stared absently out the window, confusion mixed with fear evident on her face. *She was too young to have to go through this, much too young. And if she were to lose her daddy*—Harmony nearly gasped, her gaze flicking forward to focus on the road.

She couldn't think like that. They couldn't lose Kyle; none of them could. They all needed him too much for that. When they arrived at the hospital, Harmony wrapped Lily in a warm embrace.

"It'll be okay," she whispered. It had to be. Harmony spent the time in the waiting room praying for Kyle's safety and recovery and praying for Ellie, that she would be comforted and that even at a young age, she would always understand God's infinite love for her. Finally, Harmony prayed for herself. She was in love with Kyle, but she knew that she couldn't be. And she would have to live with that for the rest of her life. After what seemed like hours, though it had only been about ten minutes, a strict-looking nurse came in.

"Are you here for Kyle Taylor?"

Lily nodded. "Do you know what is wrong with him?"

The nurse nodded curtly. "Appendicitis. We suspect he was taking numerous painkillers, and it's a miracle that his appendix hasn't already ruptured."

"Is my daddy gonna be okay?"

The nurse's expression softened when she looked at Ellie. "We certainly hope so, deary. Now," she said, returning to her no-nonsense demeanor, "he has refused to be put under until he has spoken to a woman by the name of Harmony. I warn you that if his appendix bursts, it could be fatal."

Harmony stood on weak knees. "I'm Harmony." Why would he want to see her? Would he be angry? Harmony had to go; he had to have the surgery. Raising her eyes to heaven and lifting up a prayer, she followed the nurse down the hall and into surgery.

Kyle pushed the mask away from his face for the fourth time. Boy, was this nurse persistent. But no way was he going into surgery without speaking to Harmony. She had to know how he felt, just in case the worse happened.

"Kyle?" Harmony's sweet voice drifted over to him and he tried to sit up. Okay, that was a bad idea. "Kyle!" Harmony rushed to his side, leaning over him, her blond hair framing her angelic face.

"You're beautiful," Kyle muttered. In truth, the IV the nurses had already given him was starting to make him drowsy. But he wasn't about to back out now; Harmony had to know the truth.

"Um, ma'am, we really need to be getting him down to surgery." Spoilsport.

"Oh, yes, of course." No, no, no. She couldn't leave. Yet Kyle didn't think he'd be able to explain everything before the persistent nurse lady rushed him off to surgery and away from Harmony. But really, what was there to tell?

"Harmony, I love you."

"It's okay, Kyle. We just need to get you through surgery. Don't worry, okay? Just hang on."

She must not have understood him.

"Harmony, I love you," he repeated insistently.

"Kyle, it's the drugs. Just don't worry, okay?"

Kyle frowned. Now she was just being difficult.

"Harmony," he reached up, touching her hair and feeling the silkiness of it as it slid through his fingers. He slipped his hand to the back of her neck and pulled her gently down towards him. Their lips met, and Kyle couldn't have cared less about the hospital or the pain in his gut or anything; he only cared about Harmony and this moment. When he broke the kiss, he whispered, "I love you," as the anxious nurse placed the mask over his face and everything went dark.

Harmony stumbled back out of the way as the young nurse pushed Kyle away and down the hall. Harmony touched her lips, almost giddy with excitement. Kyle had kissed her. Kyle loved her. Harmony could barely control her erratic heartbeat or slightly laboured breathing. Kyle loved her. She loved Kyle. It was absolutely perfect. Almost.

Harmony's sudden sadness counteracted every smidgen of joy. Oh boy, was she in trouble. She couldn't marry Kyle, couldn't love him. How could they make a life together if they didn't have the same values? And then there was the surgery. What if something went wrong? Harmony found tears smarting her eyes. Why did she have to fall in love with someone that she could never be with, that she could never really love?

"Oh, God, why?"

Why did she always get so close to love, only to have it snatched away? Harmony wasn't sure her heart would survive another break. All she wanted to do was curl up into a ball and find somewhere to go and cry. But she had to be strong. For Ellie.

Harmony rejoined the group, deciding it would be best if she left right then. Ellie had her grandmother and her aunt. Why should Harmony stay and torment herself? Marjorie and Lily were shocked.

"You want to leave us now?" Marjorie look so betrayed, Harmony felt the need to explain herself.

"It would probably be best for everyone if I'm not here when Kyle wakes up."

Lily folded her arms across her chest and looked pointedly at Ellie. "You're really going to leave Ellie at one of the most difficult points in her life? You're going to leave when her father is in the hospital and the only other person she loves just as much is you? You're really going to leave her?"

Harmony looked at the scared, confused expression on Ellie's face as she clutched her pink bunny tightly to her chest.

"Well," Harmony wanted to stay, but she was worried that she would only dig herself into an even deeper hole. And she would do it gladly. "I suppose I could stay until he is out of the hospital."

Lily and Marjorie thanked her gratefully and she sank down into the chair next to Ellie, letting the tired little girl lay her head in her lap. As she looked down on the sleeping girl, she realized that she wouldn't be able to leave, at least not without leaving her heart behind. And that was a big problem.

*****

Harmony had never been happier to step into the hospital on Saturday morning after hearing the good news. Kyle was all right. Harmony felt as though she was floating on air as she walked down the hall of the hospital hand-in-hand with Ellie.

Everyone was going in to see Kyle in turns. Ellie was going with Marjorie, then Lily was going, and finally, Harmony. Harmony had mixed feelings about seeing Kyle. She wanted to tell him how worried she had been, how much she cared. And yet she knew she would be walking down a path that would only lead to more heartbreak and sadness. Why did life have to be so hard?

When it was Harmony's turn to go see Kyle, she nearly bolted. *It's okay,* she reasoned. *I'll go in to see how he's doing then leave, and everything will be fine.* When she entered the room, her heart flipped over. How could anyone look that great while sitting in a hospital bed after having surgery? When he smiled at her, she suddenly felt like she was the only woman in the world. How did he do that?

"Kyle," Harmony sat herself on the chair beside his bed, "how are you feeling?" They made small talk for a while, but Kyle fidgeted with the bedsheets and couldn't seem to really focus. Finally, she asked him, "Kyle what's wrong?"

Kyle looked up at her, and she thought she'd drown in those chocolate-brown eyes of his.

"I just wanted to say I'm sorry," he blurted out hurriedly. "I'm sorry about what happened the other night, what I said, what I did…" Kyle wasn't looking at her, as though he was too ashamed even to acknowledge what had happened the night before. "I had no right, and I'm sorry."

Harmony felt like her cheeks were on fire. Of course, Kyle would be sorry about kissing her, about telling her he loved her. Harmony ducked her head, hating to think that she'd been so stupid.

"Don't…don't worry about it, Kyle. It's not a big deal." Harmony had to fight to keep her voice steady.

"It is a big deal," Kyle insisted. He ran his fingers through his hair in frustration. "I was so sick, I don't know what came over me."

Harmony had never been more embarrassed in her life, to think she'd kissed him back. Even though his sudden proclamation of love had been brought on by drugs and illness, she'd still…*Stupid, stupid, stupid.*

"It's okay, all right," Harmony snapped, a little harsher than she had meant. "I… I've got to go." Harmony stood up, and scrounging up all the dignity she could muster, left the room with her head held high, only to find tears sliding down her cheeks as she exited the doorway.

Chapter Twenty-Eight

Three days after the surgery, Harmony *still* hadn't come back to see him. He knew she hadn't left yet because his mother had told him so. Had he scared Harmony off when he told her how he felt about her? He still wasn't sure if she believed him. But why, oh, why would she be avoiding him? Was it because of something he'd said the first day when she came to visit him? Did his apology remind her of all the reasons why he wasn't good enough for her? Was she still angry about the awful way he'd fired her? He just couldn't understand women.

He'd *told* her he loved her and he *knew* that she felt the same way. He was certain of it. He felt a slow smile spreading across his lips when he thought about how he'd kissed her. And how she'd kissed him back. But he needed to see her and he needed to figure out a romantic way to propose while in the hospital. He just couldn't wait any longer.

There was a knock at his door. His mother had told him that they—herself, Lily and Ellie—would be back to see him later in the evening, but it was only two in the afternoon.

"Come in," he called, hoping against hope that it would be Harmony knocking at his door. It wasn't Harmony, but Kyle vaguely recognized the visitor. He just couldn't place her. The woman didn't look to be much older than he was, if she was older at all. She was wearing a long-sleeved T-shirt and jeans and her long brown hair was pulled up into a high ponytail.

"Uh…hi," Kyle wasn't exactly sure what to say to a visitor that he did not really know.

"Hi." The woman sat down in the chair next to his bed. She must have sensed his confusion because she promptly introduced herself.

"My name's Sherrie. I'm the nurse from the night you went into surgery."

Ah, that explained things. "Right, I remember you. You were the one who kept trying to stick that mask in my face."

Sherrie had the decency to blush.

"To be fair, your appendix was about to burst, so I think I was justified in my persistence."

Kyle grinned, leaning back against the pillows. "Yeah, I guess so."

Nurse Sherrie pulled a kid-sized version of his team's jersey out of her bag. "I was just wondering if maybe you wouldn't mind signing this for me. It's a gift for my nephew, and, well, you're his favourite player," she asked sheepishly, looking down at the ground. "If you're up to it, that is."

Kyle took the jersey from her hand, feeling a little awkward. It was just a bit weird to have someone who had helped operate on him sitting next to him like any ordinary guest.

"I just wanted to say," Sherrie had tears welling up in her eyes, "how much it moved me to see you tell that woman that you loved her." She sniffed. "It was so romantic."

"Yeah, well, it's not like she believed me anyway." Kyle wasn't into baring his soul to a stranger, but he needed someone to talk to. Strangely enough, that person was Nurse Sherrie. Must be the painkillers.

"But how could she not?" Sherrie cried.

Kyle had to say it felt good to have someone on his side. Even if that someone just happened to be a total stranger. Kyle shrugged, feeling utterly incapable.

"I just don't know what to do."

"Well, you can't give up!" The nurse in front of him seemed to come alive with vigor. "If you love her, you have to show her, pursue her, make her see that you're in for the long haul, that you are willing to give her a ring and pledge to stay with her for the rest of your lives." She sighed, her hands clasped over her heart. "That's what true love really is."

Kyle looked at her for a moment before deciding that she was right. That's what true love was.

"Thanks. You're right." Kyle nodded his head, an idea forming in his mind. "Hey, Sherrie," he called just as she rose to leave, "do you think you could do me a favour? And I'll need you to make a phone call."

After working out an elaborate plan with the enthusiastic night shift nurse, Sherrie, Kyle sent his mother and sister to go and get the needed supplies when Ellie, who was sitting on the bed with him, asked him a question.

"Awe, you mad about de cawd I made you?"

Kyle shook his head, holding her close. "No, sweetheart. I love the card."

"But you were mad at Miss Hawmony because of my pictures, wight?"

Kyle could have kicked himself. He should have known that Ellie would have heard, especially since he hadn't taken any care to keep his voice down when he had been so angry at Harmony. He'd been so sick he hadn't even worried about his three-year-old daughter who was just upstairs when he'd lashed out at Harmony.

"I'm not angry at her sweetheart, and I apologized and everything, but I'm going to make it right, okay?" Ellie nodded and looked up at him again, her blond curls framing her face.

"Awe, you mad at Miss Cassandwa?"

Kyle frowned. "Why would I be mad at Miss Cassandra?"

"She towd Miss Hawmony to use your cawds. I heawd her," Ellie cupped her hand around her mouth like she was telling him a secret and leaned up to his ear. "And she's not a vewy nice lady."

Kyle felt his anger building, and he found himself seeing only red. Cassandra had set Harmony up? That's what Harmony had been trying to tell him when he'd gotten so angry at her. He couldn't believe he'd lost it on her and yet it was Cassandra who had been responsible all along. Kyle didn't think that he had been angrier before in his life. How could Cassandra lie like that, set someone up, and nearly end up costing him the love of his life? Kyle shook his head. No way was he letting her get away with that. No. Way.

"Don't worry, sweetheart," he whispered to Ellie as he leaned down and kissed her forehead, "Daddy will fix everything."

*****

Harmony was sitting at home, trying to decide whether or not to start packing again when the phone rang. Harmony ran downstairs to the living room to snatch it out of its cradle.

"Hello?"

"Hello, is this the Taylor residence?" Harmony nodded and answered yes, trying to figure out where she had heard that voice before.

"This is the Calgary General hospital. There is a serious development that has taken place in regards to Kyle Taylor, and the whole family has been summoned to the hospital."

Harmony's heart sunk deeper at every word spoken in that grim voice.

"Has something happened?"

"I'm afraid it's really not something I can discuss over the phone, but I think it is vital that you get here as quickly as possible."

Harmony had hung up and was in the car, driving down the highway practically before the voice on the phone stopped speaking. Harmony nearly bolted down the hospital hallway to Kyle's room, praying every step of the way. *God, please let him be all right.*

When she burst through the door of Kyle's room, she stopped dead in her tracks. The lights were dimmed, there was a candle on the hospital table, and Kyle was sitting on the bed, holding a bouquet of ruby-red roses. Harmony took one look in the room and backed out the doors.

"Harmony? Harmony, come back!"

Oh, so she did have the right room. Harmony reentered the room slowly, unsure of what to expect. Kyle held the roses out to her with a grin that would have challenged the sun.

"These are for you."

Harmony took them warily, wondering what on earth was going on. Harmony smiled down at the bouquet of roses in her hands.

They really were beautiful. When Harmony looked up, she gasped. Kyle was smiling at her, holding a blue velvet ring box that contained a sparkling diamond engagement ring.

"Harmony," Kyle looked at her with those expressive brown eyes, "will you marry me?"

Every cell in her body screamed yes. She could almost hear herself uttering the words. Harmony shook her head as tears ran down her cheeks. She couldn't marry him. She just couldn't.

Kyle felt his chest tighten as he saw Harmony shaking her head. He couldn't lose her now. Had he misread everything? Didn't she love him? Couldn't she at least try to love him?

"Harmony…why?"

He had to know why; he wasn't letting her go without a fight. Harmony shook her head again, wiping the tears as they ran down her face.

"I… I can't tell you."

"What do you mean you can't tell me?" Kyle ran his hand through his hair, trying not to let the frustration he was feeling colour his words.

"I just can't marry you. I wish I could, but I can't." Harmony shook her head again, tears streaming down her cheeks.

"But Harmony," he pleaded, "I love you." Harmony looked startled at his words, and for a moment, she just looked at him. Then she shook her head.

"But you said you were sorry for telling me you loved me, for… for kissing me."

Now it was Kyle's turn to shake his head. "I'm not sorry for that at all. I was sorry about how angry and mean I was to you before I left for the game that night."

Harmony looked up, relief evident in her features. Then she started crying again, and Kyle felt like his heart was ripping into two.

"But Harmony, I love you. I want to spend my whole life making you happy and loving you like Christ loves the church." He ran his hand through his hair again. He had to get her to change her mind. Harmony looked at him, her gaze filled with surprise.

"How do you know about all that, about Christ loving the church?"

"Well, because I've started reading my Bible," he said it like it was obvious, but he realized he hadn't told anyone but Scott and Lucas that he had become a Christian.

"Why would you be doing that?" Harmony's expression was wary, but he caught a glimmer of hope in her eyes. Kyle could suddenly see exactly where she was coming from. A "lopsided" marriage wouldn't stand the test of time. Harmony didn't know that Christ was now the center of Kyle's life like He was of hers.

"I… I became a Christian a couple weeks ago, and I didn't tell you because," Kyle sighed, "I was hoping you would notice."

"That's why you were acting so different," Harmony muttered to herself wonderingly. Kyle looked at her again, holding out the ring box once again.

"So, Harmony…will you make me the happiest man alive and let me spend the rest of my life loving you? Will you marry me and be my wife until death do us part?"

Harmony smiled through her tears before launching herself into his arms.

"Yes!"

For a moment, Kyle just sat there holding her, letting the meaning of her words seep into his soul. She'd said yes. She was going to marry him.

"I love you, Harmony." He cupped her face in his hands and kissed her hair, her cheeks, and her soft lips…"I love you so much."

Harmony smiled at him, the love in her gaze warming him to the core.

"I love you too."

Epilogue

Harmony was sitting on the couch with her feet up and a notebook on her lap. She couldn't help gazing admiringly at the ring Kyle had given her. It suited her perfectly, set in white gold with one medium-sized diamond at the center and a bunch of tiny channel set diamonds on both sides. It was beautiful.

She refocused on writing the guest list only to find that she had lost her pen. At that moment, Kyle walked into the living room, looking as strong and as handsome as ever. Harmony felt her heart jump. This was the man she would be spending her life with.

"Hello, gorgeous," Kyle greeted her, taking his place beside her on the couch. "What are you writing?"

"Guest list," Harmony answered. "Or at least I was, before I lost my pen."

Kyle smirked, pulling the pen from behind her ear. "This pen?"

Harmony blushed scarlet and snatched the pen from his hand. "Thank you," she said pertly. "How's the hunt for a new agent going?" she asked him, writing some more names down on her notepad.

"Amazingly enough, I seem to be a bit of a hot commodity in the hockey world, and it looks like I'm going to have my pick of agents."

Harmony smiled. "That's great, Kyle." Then, giving him a playful elbow in the ribs, she added, "Isn't it nice to be wanted?"

Kyle chuckled. "So, what do you have planned so far?" Kyle asked her, looking over her shoulder to read her notebook.

"Well," Harmony began, "I was thinking of having a small wedding. Not too many people, just close family and friends." Harmony looked up at him. "How does that sound?"

Kyle grinned, "Whatever makes you happy, makes me happy."

Harmony smiled, thanking God for the man He had given her. "You are the most wonderful man I could ever hope to marry. I love you." She looked at him again. "Kyle, what is it?"

Kyle didn't meet her gaze at first, running one hand through his hair and pulling her close with the other.

"Are you sure you don't want a big wedding? We could wait and have a big summer wedding and a long honeymoon. I don't want you to have to compromise because of the hockey season."

Harmony had to resist rolling her eyes. They had had this conversation nearly a thousand times.

"A Christmas wedding is exactly what I want, and besides, I'll have my whole life to spend with you." She sighed, leaning into him. "I don't need a honeymoon."

"It's a lot to get together in such a short time. Are you sure you don't need more time?"

Harmony nodded. "I'll be fine, don't worry. It'll be fun." She smiled and raised her face for a kiss. Kyle gladly obliged.

"Well," he said, brown eyes twinkling, "really, that's a good thing. I don't think I could wait till summer to marry you."

Harmony smiled again. "Well, you're a lucky man," she said laughingly, "because you won't have to."

About the Author

Cassidy Lea is a young woman with a desire to know God more each day and to honour Him in all she does. She is an all-Canadian girl who loves spending time with family and friends, going to hockey games, and of course, writing!

Cassidy especially loves reading and writing romance novels, and it is her prayer that God will use her writing to touch the hearts of many.

CPSIA information can be obtained
at www.ICGtesting.com
Printed in the USA
LVHW031956240121
677374LV00019B/774